WINTER'S CRIMES 24

WINTER'S CRIMES
24

EDITED BY
MARIA REJT

MACMILLAN

LONDON

First published 1992 by Macmillan London Limited
a division of Pan Macmillan Publishers Limited
Cavaye Place London SW10 9PG
and Basingstoke

Associated companies throughout the world

ISBN 0-333-58468-6

1 3 5 7 9 8 6 4 2

A CIP catalogue record for this book is available from
the British Library

Phototypeset by Intype, London
Printed by Mackays of Chatham PLC, Chatham, Kent

CONTENTS

EDITOR'S NOTE

Poised on the brink of its twenty-fifth year, *Winter's Crimes* continues to uphold the outstanding tradition of the series, with original stories commissioned to offer the reader the very best in crime fiction. Last year I inherited the editor's mantle and, once again, I am delighted to introduce our ten authors. Some are new contributors, others have written stories for *Winter's Crimes* before. It has given me enormous pleasure to bring them together in a collection of amazing variety and tantalizing ingenuity. My heartfelt thanks to them all!

COLIN DEXTER

'Let those who lament the decline of the English detective
story reach for Colin Dexter.'

MONTY'S REVOLVER

IT WASN'T often that Professor Rawlins bothered her with his personal letters. Occasionally, though – like this afternoon; and like yesterday afternoon, come to think of it. But he always insisted on putting his own stamps on such letters, never allowing them through the Department's franking-machine. Bit too obviously self-righteous, she thought. She glanced at the tiny gold watch (a wedding present) on her left wrist: almost a quarter to five. TGFF. Thank God For Friday!

Rawlins took off his half-glasses, pinched the top of his nose, turned over a page of his desk diary, lit another cigarette, and looked across at Carol Summerson.

'Professor Smithson's coming on Monday morning. Will you nip out first thing and get me a bottle of Glenfiddich?'

Carol made a note, closed her shorthand book, uncrossed her elegant legs, and smiled as she looked at him. And he, half smiling himself, looked back across at her; and she felt pleasingly surprised. (Or was it surprisingly pleased?) There had been so few moments of real communication between them during the three months she'd been working for him – the man she'd more than once heard described as 'the cleverest fellow in Oxford'.

She was glad to get out of his office, though. He would never open the window and the smell in the room was invariably horrid. How she wished he'd stop smoking! (John never smoked, thank goodness.) How old was he? Sixty? Overweight, and with a chest that sounded like a loose-strung harp, he was just the sort to die before his time from heart trouble or lung cancer or chronic bronchitis or emphysema – or like as not the whole lot of them listed on his death certificate. Why didn't his *wife* do something about him, for Christ's sake?

'Good night, sir,' she heard herself say; and for a moment she fancied that she'd almost like to look after him herself.

John was waiting for her, sitting on his wife's swivel-chair and turning over the papers that lay on her desk. (He always picked Carol up on Fridays.) While she was out in the cloak-room, he looked through a few more recent carbons, each neatly stapled to its originating letter. One carbon in particular caught his eye:

Dear Jack,

Glad you still remember me and – yes! – I still keep the old collection going. But anything that belonged to Monty is sure to spark off some keen bidding – all a bit too high for me. As you say, though, the reserve price seems fair enough.

How long is it since we met? Seven – eight years? Marion died six years ago – malignant tumour. Not unexpected, but all desperately sad and very upsetting for the boys. I remarried two years later, and since then I've had another son! – and another!! – and another!!! Do you know the odds against a penny coming down *six* times on the trot?

If you're ever near Oxford, let me know. I promise not to show you around the Department.

Sincerely yours,

Carol looked at her husband as she re-entered her office. At twenty-two, he was a year younger than herself; yet in many ways since their marriage two years previously, he'd shown himself the more mature, the more dependable, of the two. There had been a few patches of squabbling – mostly her fault; and the one continuing sadness . . . But she was glad she'd married him.

That, at least, is what Carol Summerson was telling herself that December afternoon.

4

'You reading my boss's correspondence again?'

He nodded.

'Interesting?'

'Not really.'

As she unhooked her coat from the wall-cupboard, John glanced quickly at the originating letter, stapled behind the carbon he had just been reading. A letterhead announced a 'J. Wingate, Gunsmith', with an address in Guildford, the letter itself reporting the forthcoming auction of a revolver that had belonged to Field Marshal Bernard Montgomery – reserve price: £3,000.

'I didn't know he was interested in revolvers,' said John, unlocking the nearside door to the Metro.

'I've told you *before*. You shouldn't read—'

'Didn't mind, did you?'

'Course not!' She brushed her full lips against his cheek as she fastened her safety-belt.

'His big hobby. One of the girls went to his house once when he'd got bronchitis or something and she said he'd got all these revolvers like in cases sort of thing hanging round the walls. Not very nice really, is it? You'd think that with all those young children—'

She stopped suddenly and a silence fell between them.

At 5.20 p.m. Rawlins locked the door of his office and left the Department. Florence (at thirty-two, exactly half his age) would have the fish all ready. TGFF. Thank God For Florence!

That night, for no immediately apparent reason, Frank Rawlins dreamed of Carol Summerson.

It was just before 11 a.m. the following Monday that Smithson arrived. Carol was not introduced to him, but from her adjacent room she could hear his voice; could hear, too, the occasional gurgle of Glenfiddich and the clink of the office glasses. Just over an hour later, after the pair of them had walked past her window, she entered Rawlins' office, took the two glasses, washed them out in the ladies' loo, and bent down to put them back in the cupboard beside the bottle – now empty.

'Hallo!'

She hadn't heard him come back in, and she felt slightly confused as he steered her by the elbow into her own office.

'Don't you think it's about time I treated my confidential secretary to lunch?'

He looked – and sounded – surprisingly sober; and she felt flattered. Soon he was holding her coat ready, and she was slipping her arms into the sleeves.

Easily.

He was interesting – no doubt about that. He told her of the time he and Smithson had worked together in a VD clinic in Vienna; and as he reminisced of this and other experiences Carol felt herself enriched, and newly important.

'Another?'

'I've had enough, thank you.'

'Nonsense!' He picked up her glass and made his slightly unsteady way to the bar once more.

Her third gin-and-tonic tasted strong. Nice, though! Was it a double? His own drink looked very much like the orange-juice he'd promised himself; and after he'd left her to visit the gents' she took a sip of it: it tasted even more strongly of gin than hers.

'We'd better be getting back, sir.'

'Yes.'

'Thanks for a lovely lunch.'

'Carol! I've had a lot to drink – you know that. But I just want you to know how ver' much I'd like to go to bed with you this afternoon.'

Carol's heart sank.

'Don't be silly! Come on, let's get back!'

He was hurt, she knew that; a bit ashamed, too. And as they walked back he tried so very hard to sound his usual sober self.

That night Carol Summerson dreamed of Frank Rawlins.

Erotically.

Carol's rise came through in mid-January, and she was thrilled.

'I'm ever so grateful, sir.'

'You deserve it.'

'Will you come out one day and have lunch with *me*?'

'When?'

'Whenever you're free.'

'Today?'

'Today!'

She saw to it that he drank almost all the wine, and she insisted on buying him a glass of brandy after their meal. They were sitting close together now, and gently she moved her right leg against the rough tweed of his trousers. And, just as gently, he responded, saying nothing, yet saying everything.

'Another brandy?' she ventured.

Rawlins looked down at his empty glass, and smiled a little sadly.

'Have you ever thought how wonderful it would be to have a quiet, civilised little place all to yourself where—'

He stopped, and there was a long silence between them before Carol spoke softly in his ear.

'But I've *got* a nice little place out at Wheatley. You see, John's away for a few days . . .'

Seven weeks later, Carol's GP told her that she was quite definitely pregnant.

On the Friday evening of that same week, John Summerson called as usual to collect his wife. It was quarter-to-five – exactly so – when he walked through into Rawlins' office and sat down in the chair that his wife had just vacated.

Over his glasses, Rawlins' eyes registered puzzlement: it was as though a new boy had just strolled into the Masters' Common Room.

'Can I help you? John – isn't it?'

'You had sex with my wife.' Summerson spoke quietly, firmly – defying all denial.

'Where on earth did you get such—?'

'You're lying!'

'Look here! You can't be serious—'

'She's pregnant!'

'But you can't—'

'I *watched* you!' hissed Summerson.

'But you—'

'Shut up! I'm not the father. I can *never* be a father. You do understand what I'm saying, don't you?'

'Yes,' answered Rawlins softly.

'Did you *enjoy* it?' The young man's eyes were blazing with a terrible anguish.

'I just—'

'*Shut up!*'

Rawlins sank back in his chair, his shoulders sagging.

'I'm redundant now,' continued Summerson. 'They gave me £3,000 for the five years I worked there. There's not *much* you can do with £3,000, is there, Professor?'

Rawlins closed his eyes and thought of his sons and thought of Florence and thought of himself, too: he knew exactly what £3,000 might possibly have bought.

When he opened his eyes he saw the revolver in Summerson's right hand – a British Enfield .380, Number 2, Mark 1, the wooden stock a dirty nicotine-brown, the gunmetal of the fluted barrel as clean and gleaming as a polished stone. Summerson swivelled the revolver round until it pointed straight at Rawlins' heart, and his finger squeezed the trigger until the hammer lifted to the limit of the catch.

'Pretty accurate, they tell me, at such close range as this, Professor!'

Rawlins said nothing, his eyes seemingly mesmerised as he stared at the cylinder-chamber. But now the revolver was no longer pointing at him; for with slow deliberation Summerson turned it round upon himself and brought the tip of the shining barrel up against his own right temple, where the index finger of his right hand finally exacted that minimal extra pressure on the double-action trigger, and the hammer drove against the cylinder-chamber.

The children had eaten half an hour previously, and Florence Rawlins looked down sadly at the juiceless fillet that lay beneath the low-burning grill. Why couldn't Frank be more thoughtful?

Six o'clock.
Ten past.
Twenty past.
At half-past six she rang his private office-number, but there was no reply.

'Fine! Fine!' The young gynaecologist had repeated. 'No problems. Now you'll promise not to smoke, won't you?' 'I promise.' Of course she wouldn't smoke! Her thoughts drifted back happily to Rawlins . . . With a father like Rawlins, it would surely be a *boy* – and pretty certainly a *clever* little boy, at that! She'd longed to be a mother ever since she'd been a young girl, when she'd played incessantly, obsessively almost, with her dollies – dressing them, combing their lank locks, bending their stiff joints before propping them up against the backs of chairs . . .

Six weeks after that first antenatal clinic, an oblong parcel was delivered to the Rawlins' residence, where later in the day the Professor of Forensic Medicine inspected its contents with enthusiasm. The new case would naturally take pride of place, perhaps just inside the front entrance, he thought. He fitted the revolver carefully inside the specially constructed case, closed the glass cover, and held the exhibit up against some imaginary hook on the facing wall. Not a bad reward, really, for being trapped into exercising his dubiously enviable knack of procreating male offspring with even the most perfunctory ejaculation. And even that extraordinary afternoon when young Summerson had pointed the revolver at his heart hadn't been all that traumatic an experience really, because long before the final, cosmically anticlimatic 'click' he had known (as any expert in the field would have known) that there were no bullets in the open chambers of the revolver – not a single one. For all that though, it had been a great relief when the revolver had at last been lowered, and a genuine surprise when Summerson had presented it to him across the desk – reward for services rendered, so to speak. And he really *had* needed those two large whiskies, although he'd afterwards agreed with a worried, tearful Florence that he should have told her he'd be late.

On September 29 of that same year, a baby was delivered on the third floor of the Maternity Hospital up at Headington, and the young father had the name all ready. The gunsmith from Guildford may not have bothered to work out any mathematical odds, but John Summerson had calculated the chances of a penny coming down heads for a *seventh* time; and at 128:1, they'd seemed to him wildly improbable.

They called the lovely little girl 'Francesca'.

ELIZABETH
FERRARS

'The doyenne of English crime writers since
Agatha Christie.'

STOP THIEF!

ROGER GATES put the mowing-machine away in the garden shed. Coming out of the shed and closing its door, he stood still for a moment, drawing in one or two deep breaths. The air was full of the scent of new-mown grass, the most exquisite scent, he thought, in the world. Today had been the first time that he had mown the grass since the winter. For the last months he had occasionally managed to find a little work to do in the garden, but this Saturday morning had been the first time since the end of November that he had been able to spend some hours exerting himself fully, surrounded on all sides by the lovely beginnings of springtime.

The forsythia was a burst of yellow at the bottom of the garden. The early clematis, hanging in great clumps on the wooden fence that surrounded the garden, was a glory of tender pink. The daffodils that crowded thickly in the beds that bordered the neat lawn that he had just finished mowing were at their best. The aubretia in thick cushions of purple brightened the rockery. Even the pasque-flowers were in the midst of their brief flowering. After the meagre patches of colour given to the garden during the winter by the yellow jasmine and the winter-flowering cherry, there was a wealth of it that filled Roger with deep content. There had never been anything imaginative in the design of the garden, but simply a richness of blossoming, specially in this lovely month.

Going to the back door of the house, through which he always came out into the garden, he pushed it open, stepped inside and climbed out of the wellingtons that he had been wearing. His slippers were there where he had left them when he went out, beside the doormat. He put them on and was just about to go to the sink to wash his hands when an extraordinary thing struck him. On the table was a packet of cigarettes.

His wife, Coralie, had never smoked and he himself had not smoked for ten years.

He looked at the packet with a puzzled frown, wondering how it could have got where it was. Then a possible explanation struck him and when he had washed his hands he walked along the passage to the living-room, where, as he had expected, he found Coralie and said cheerfully, 'Hallo, have we had a visitor?'

But Coralie was not quite in the state that he had expected. He had thought that he would find her sitting by the fire with sherry and glasses on a tray by her side, waiting for him. But although she was sitting by the fire, there was no sherry there and she did not look round at him when he came in. Instead she simply stared with a curious blankness into the fire. Also she was wearing her overcoat and her fur-lined boots, as if she had only just got in from her visit to the village shop. But he knew that she had set out even before he had started out into the garden and that had been over two hours ago. The only explanation that he could think of was that she had stopped in at some neighbour's house for a coffee and had only just got home. But that did not explain why she had brought cigarettes back with her.

Coralie was forty, three years younger than he was himself. She was a slender, delicate-looking woman, with smooth fair hair that she wore brushed straight back from her face and coiled into a loose knot on her neck. Her face was oval, still pale from a recent illness, with grey eyes fringed with long lashes, and to Roger she was as beautiful as when he had met her first. That had been six years ago. They had got married only three months after that meeting and together had chosen this house in the village of Lexlade, which was three miles from the town of Allingford, where Roger had recently been appointed manager in the bank in different branches of which, in different parts of the country, he had spent all his working life. It had been a deep satisfaction to him to arrive in Allingford, for it had been a return to where life had begun for him. He had been born there, had been educated in its comprehensive and had had his first very junior job there.

Coralie was a Londoner and still liked to spend an occasional day in London, having lunch with some old friend and doing a little shopping, but, like him, she had fallen in love with the charming house in the village and had entered with enthusiasm into village activities. Not that she had been able to take much part in them for the last two months, for she had had a difficult time recovering from her illness. It was taking much longer than anyone had anticipated. But of course at forty it was not to be expected that she would recover like a young woman from the danger and tragedy of a very painful miscarriage.

He repeated what he had said as he came into the room. 'Have we had a visitor?'

She turned her head to look at him with a vagueness that he was startled to find a little frightening.

'Not that I know of,' she said.

'No one's been in to see us this morning?' he asked.

'Not unless it was while I was out shopping. Why?'

'Ah, perhaps that's what it was. You were out shopping and I was in the garden and . . .' But it did not feel right. 'It's just those cigarettes on the kitchen table. I wondered how they got there.'

'Oh.' There was concentration in her great eyes, the vagueness had gone. 'Yes, of course you saw them.'

'Well, how did they get there? I mean, did someone leave them, or did you get them for someone, or what?'

'I don't know,' she said. 'I – I found them.'

'Found them in the kitchen?'

'No, in my pocket. My coat pocket.' She patted the pocket of the coat that she was still wearing. 'In here.'

'But when?' He was bewildered.

'After I came out of the shop. I put my hand in my pocket to get my handkerchief and there they were.'

'I don't understand,' he said. 'How did they get there?'

'I don't know.' Her voice was dull, as if she were not much interested. She stood up. 'I'll get the sherry.'

'Just a minute,' he said. 'You don't mean you think someone slipped them into your pocket as a kind of trick?'

'There was no one else in the shop. No, of course I took them myself, but I don't know why.'

She left the room and after a few minutes returned without her overcoat and having changed from her boots into slippers, and carrying a tray with the sherry and glasses on it.

In a strange way it disturbed Roger more that she looked entirely her normal self than it would have if she had shown some sign of mental disturbance, for while she had been out of the room he had been trying to make himself face the fact that the aftermath of that miscarriage might perhaps be a breakdown of some kind. Once or twice during the last few weeks he had feared it, but her occasional fits of strangeness had always passed off quite quickly and he had hoped that they were at an end.

She poured out the sherry, sank back in her chair by the fire and smiled.

'Did you have a nice morning in the garden?' she asked.

'Yes, yes, but did you pay for them, Coralie? The cigarettes.'

'How could I when I didn't know I had them?' She laughed. 'Anyhow, one packet of cigarettes, they won't miss them.'

He sat down in the chair facing hers across the fireplace, sipped his sherry and fell silent.

Next morning she would not go to church with him. She said that she had slept very badly and had a headache, but when he suggested that he should stay at home with her she was very insistent that he should go as usual. When the service was over the vicar, who stood outside the doorway chatting to his parishioners as they left, asked him if Mrs Gates was not well. All Lexlade knew of her illness, just as they had known before it of the somewhat surprising fact that in her middle age she had become pregnant.

'Thank you,' Roger said. 'Not too grand, as a matter of fact. But she just needs a bit of rest. It's nothing to worry about.'

'And that job in London,' the vicar said. 'Have you made up your mind about it? Are you leaving us?'

'Good Lord, no. Not for anything.' The news that Roger had been offered an appointment as manager of a bank in

Battersea had somehow spread through the village, though he had hardly given it a thought. Of course it would have meant promotion and a higher salary, though the advantages of that might have been cancelled by the increased cost of living in London. But it would also have meant leaving the small community in which he had lived very happily for these last few years, and the garden that now was really repaying all the hard work that he had put into it. But it had to be admitted that the way that the rumour had spread was his own fault. He had boasted about the offer to one or two people over drinks in the Red Lion. Perhaps, though he could not remember doing so, he had spoken about it to the vicar himself.

'Well, I'm delighted to hear it,' the vicar said. 'You'd have been sorely missed here. And please give my best wishes to Mrs Gates.'

Roger went on through the old churchyard to the gateway and across the village green to his home. As he went he wondered what Coralie had done with the packet of cigarettes and on an impulse, before going into the house, he looked into the dustbin that stood beside the back door. The packet was there, which on the whole relieved him.

It was two days later that the second packet of cigarettes appeared.

Like the one before, he found it on the kitchen table when he returned in the evening from the bank in Allingford. He had just put the car away in the garage and taken a short stroll round the garden, enjoying the wonderful softly scented sense of returning life around him, then he went into the house, as usual when he had been in the garden, by the back door, and saw the cigarettes on the table before him.

A different brand this time, he thought. Not that he was up to date about such things nowadays, but the packet looked different. He suddenly became aware of a faintly sick feeling. He might have put the thing in the dustbin straight away, but found that he felt an extraordinary reluctance to touch it. He felt a similar reluctance to talk about it when he went into the sitting-room and found Coralie in her usual chair, quietly knitting. She had always done a good deal of knitting and was very skilled at it, a result of which was an accumulation of jerseys and cardigans, some of them for him, in the chest of drawers in their bedroom.

She looked up at him and smiled and said, 'Had a good day?'

It was all so normal that it seemed silly to be bothering about a packet of cigarettes. All the same, when he had kissed her and sat down, he said, 'Taking up smoking?'

She looked puzzled. 'Smoking?'

'Yes,' he said, 'I see you've been buying cigarettes again.'

'Oh,' she said, 'those.'

'Well,' he said, 'if you really want to smoke, why don't you?'

'I don't,' she said. 'I thought I'd give them to Mrs Banks.'

Mrs Banks was their daily help. She came in to clean the house on five mornings a week and enjoyed a cup of tea and a cigarette halfway through her three hours work. She was also responsible, to some extent, for spreading the news of such things as Coralie's pregnancy and later miscarriage throughout the village. She was a very efficient and friendly woman and Coralie claimed that she was entirely dependent on her.

'I thought you didn't much like her smoking in the kitchen,' Roger said. 'Didn't you try to get her to eat a biscuit instead?'

'You can't change people.'

'Well, it's a change in you, actually buying her cigarettes for her.' He hesitated. 'You did buy them, I suppose? I mean, it wasn't like last time, you didn't just find them in your pocket?'

'I think I found them in my basket. Yes, I'm sure I did. It doesn't matter, does it?'

'No, but you did pay for them, didn't you?'

'I think so. I expect I did.'

'Surely you know.'

She gave an irritated frown. 'How can one be sure when they rattle all the prices off on that computer thing? One can't think of everything.'

'Coralie, I don't believe you did pay for them. Darling, please be honest with me. Didn't you just help yourself to them for some – oh, some very peculiar sort of reason, but one we ought to talk about. I only want to help.'

She stood up, dropped her knitting into the basket on the

floor at her side and walked out of the room.

He could hear that she went into the kitchen and set about preparing their evening meal. Presently, as usual, she came in with the sherry, then dished up the veal casserole that she had cooked earlier and a chocolate mousse. Her cooking was as good as ever, but she was very silent and would not meet his eyes. Afterwards, when she had set the dishwasher going, she switched on the television without asking him if the programme was one that he wanted to watch, which as it happened it was not, and then sat in front of it for the rest of the evening. She went early to bed. Before following her, Roger went out to the kitchen and saw that the cigarettes had vanished. Like the first packet, he found them in the dustbin.

Next morning, on his way into Allingford, he called in at the village shop, which he was able to do because it opened half an hour before he was due at the bank. It was run by a middle-aged couple called McQueen, who in spite of their name had never been in Scotland, yet took a certain pride in their remote Scottish ancestry. Bob McQueen did the ordering for the shop, saw to the two local weekly deliveries and looked after the accounts. Katie, his wife, ran the shop, which was a well-organised self-service place, answered the telephone, took orders and got to know the customers.

The shop was almost empty when Roger entered it. One woman whom he knew by sight, though he could not remember her name, was studying the shelf of canned soups. He and she said good morning to one another, though he doubted if she knew who he was any more than he knew her. As he approached Katie McQueen, who was seated at the counter that had the computer on it, she looked up at him with what he thought was a trace of anxiety in her smile. He did not often appear in the shop.

'Good morning, Mrs McQueen,' he said. 'How are you?'

'Very well thank you, Mr Gates,' she answered. 'And how are you?'

'Fine, fine,' he said. 'I just called in because my wife thinks she didn't pay for some cigarettes she got here yesterday. She may be mistaken, but she wanted me to make sure of it.'

Katie McQueen's smile brightened and the anxiety faded from it.

'That's very thoughtful of her,' she said. 'Yes, I thought there was a bit of a mix-up about that, though I didn't really like to say anything about it. It would have been so embarrassing if I was wrong. Or if I was right, come to think of it. But thank you for settling the matter. How is she now?'

She was certainly one of the people who knew of the miscarriage.

'Oh, getting along pretty well, thank you,' he said. 'Gets tired pretty quickly still, but that's only to be expected.'

'That's right. My first was a miscarriage, you know, and it nearly broke my heart. I got sort of muddled and confused after it, I remember. It was very hard for Bob. But then Ian came along and everything went all right.'

In fact the McQueens had had four children after the first failure. The eldest was at Bristol University, studying law, the second was apprenticed to a builder in Allingford and the next two went on the school bus into Allingford every morning to the comprehensive. But the McQueens had married young. There would be no Ian for Coralie.

Roger paid what she owed for the cigarettes and went on to the bank.

When he returned home that evening he did not go straight into the house but again lingered for a little while in the garden, pulling out a weed here and there and noticing how swiftly the grass on the strip of lawn seemed to be growing now and that it would be able to do with another cut at the weekend. Then, with a slight sigh, he entered the house by the kitchen door.

There were no cigarettes on the table today, but there was a tin of baby food.

A feeling of painful pity flooded him. In his insensitive way, he thought, he had not understood how much the loss of her child had meant to Coralie. He had not troubled to understand.

When he went into the sitting-room and found her in her usual chair, knitting, and she asked him cheerfully if he had had a good day, he nodded his head and kissed her on the cheek and said nothing about the baby food. But he had a feeling that she found something unsatisfactory in this. Could it be, he wondered, that she had wanted to be scolded for having done something so foolish as buying it, or bringing it home, that was to say, perhaps without having paid for it? For he felt certain, though he could not have said why, that she had not paid for it. The tin was only little and would easily have slipped unnoticed into her coat pocket.

But that was something that he could not allow, even if he said nothing to Coralie about it. He could not let it be said that his wife was shop-lifting. He would have to make some arrangement with Mrs McQueen.

Next morning, as he had the day before, he went into the shop on his way into Allingford. The same other customer was there who had been there yesterday. Someone, he supposed, who did her shopping early before going on to her work, whatever it was. But this morning she smiled at him and said, 'Good morning, Mr Gates, I hope your doing her shopping for Mrs Gates doesn't mean she's had a relapse.'

He wished that he could remember her name. He was fairly sure that they had met at some village function. He also wished very much that she was not there. It would have made it easier to talk to Mrs McQueen.

But she took the initiative. Looking sympathetic, she said, 'I know why you're here, Mr Gates, and of course you're right, we'll have to do something about it, we can't just let it go on, can we? I don't mean I don't understand and I'll do anything I can to help, but I actually saw her do it, you know. Just slipped the thing into her pocket as if she didn't mind if I saw her or not. And then when I spoke to her about it and suggested quite pleasantly she'd forgotten to pay and wouldn't it be best if she did, she just looked kind of puzzled and said she didn't know what I was talking about. And not wanting a scene with other customers in the shop, I didn't argue but let her get away with it. But I can't just let it go on, now can I?'

The other customer had moved up close to the desk and was waiting to pay for her own purchases.

'No, no, of course not,' Roger said, 'and I think you've been very kind so far, and of course I'm going to discuss it with her, but meantime if you'd just keep a note of what we owe you and let me settle up when I come in, I'm sure that'll be the best thing to do.'

He hoped that that was not so explicit that the other customer could be sure of what he was talking about.

'That'll be quite all right, and I hate to worry you about it,' Mrs McQueen said, 'but if I was you I'd talk it over with a doctor. Do you have Dr Bayliss? He's ever so understanding. Thanks—' This was as Roger handed her a five-pound note and she pounded the amount on her computer and gave him the change. 'Good morning, Liz dear.'

This was to the woman standing behind him, Liz Linklater. He suddenly remembered her name and who she was. He remembered her perfectly now. She ran a small hairdressing salon in the village to which Coralie went about once a fortnight and where, she said, more local gossip was to be heard in the hour or so that she spent there than anywhere else. Roger had met the woman at a fête that was held every year in the summer, where she had been in charge of one of the stalls. Saying a sheepish good-morning to her, he hurried out of the shop, thinking, however, that Mrs McQueen had given him good advice. He would talk the situation over with Matthew Bayliss, who was quite a good friend of his.

He telephoned him soon after reaching his office and they arranged to have lunch together in the small Indian restaurant that was almost opposite the bank. Matthew Bayliss was a member of a group practice in Allingford, but he lived in Lexlade and twice a week held a surgery there. It was one of his Lexlade mornings and Roger had had to telephone him at the village hall, part of which was given over to him. They met and ordered their curry and beer and made a few remarks about the pleasant spring weather, in spite of which, according to Bayliss, flu was raging in the neighbourhood. Then Roger, dropping his voice as if he were afraid that someone might be spying on them, said that he hoped that Bayliss would treat what he had to say as entirely confidential.

'Naturally,' the doctor said, 'but I think I can tell you what you're going to say to me.'

'It's about Coralie—'

'And her shop-lifting, isn't it? Physically she's pretty well, it seems to me, but I realise how this other thing must be worrying you.'

Roger stared at him, shocked. 'But how have you heard about it? It isn't common knowledge, is it?'

'Rapidly becoming so, I'm afraid. I've just been to the Old Parsonage, and also it happens to be Liz Linklater's day for the place, and she seems to have picked up the story somehow.'

The Old Parsonage was an old people's home in Lexlade where Matthew Bayliss attended after his morning surgery in the village and where Liz Linklater visited once a week to wash and set the old women's hair and cut the old men's. She brought them what news she could and enjoyed a good gossip as much as they did.

'I understand,' Roger said sadly. 'She was in the shop when I was there, trying to sort things out with Mrs McQueen so that there'd be as little scandal as possible. She's been very decent about it. She's just going to let me know what Coralie owes her and not risk making a scene in the shop. And it was her idea that I should talk to you. Can you help me at all, Matthew? Can you give me any advice?'

'What's Coralie actually taken so far, that you know of?' Bayliss asked.

'Two packets of cigarettes and a tin of baby food.'

'Hm, not very much. Not very ambitious. But if she thinks she's got away with it, it might get worse. The odd box of chocolates, the bottle of wine hidden under a newspaper in her basket. And after that, who knows? I don't want to depress you unnecessarily, but if I were you I'd have it out with her. It's an obvious after-effect of the miscarriage, which at her age was a very serious matter. In its way it isn't surprising, in fact I feel we ought almost to have expected something of the sort. The main thing is she shouldn't feel you've turned against her because of it. If you like I could fix up for her to see a psychiatrist. There's a quite good man at the Infirmary. But I don't really recommend it at this stage. He won't be able to help her much until she wants to be helped. That may come, and then he might come in useful. Meantime it seems to me you've done the best you could already, I mean settling it with Mrs McQueen. That's quite important.'

'But because of that bloody Linklater woman, it's going to get all round the village.'

'I shouldn't worry about that too much. People understand these things a lot better than they used to. You'll find they're more sympathetic than you expect.'

'I don't want sympathy! I want Coralie as she used to be.'

A faintly sceptical look appeared on the doctor's face, almost as if he thought that perhaps Roger had never really known what Coralie used to be, but the look was gone in an instant.

'Anyway, you aren't thinking of moving, are you?' he said. 'You've dropped that idea.'

'Yes, I never thought of it very seriously,' Roger said. 'And I imagine it's pretty important now that we should have peace and quiet.'

He was in need of peace and quiet himself, he thought, after all the anxieties of the last few weeks, which might not have affected him as deeply as they had Coralie, but still had made heavy demands on him, and when he arrived home that evening he was in a tense and nervous state. But at least there was no sign that Coralie had acquired anything from the shop but her normal purchases and they had a peaceful time together. But he took a swift look in the dustbin and saw the tin of baby food was there. The dustmen having been round that morning the two packets of cigarettes had gone and besides the tin there was nothing in the bin but some potato peelings.

They had sherry before their meal and Roger told himself that he ought to make some attempt to discuss the matter that had been on his mind all day, but Coralie seemed to be in such a placid mood and the steak and kidney pie that she had cooked was so particularly good that it seemed a pity to risk destroying the pleasantness of the evening. They made love that night for the first time since she had returned from the hospital. One of the after-effects of her miscarriage had been a withdrawal from sex. But that night she was loving and tender, though near the end she murmured in his ear, 'I'm sorry, I'm sorry.' But whether she was sorry because she had disgraced herself in public, or because she had failed to bear his child, he could not be sure.

Whatever she had meant, he went off to Allingford in a better mood the next morning than for the last few days. He felt that there was no need to call in at the shop and once in his office devoted himself to his work with more concentration than he had managed to achieve since the weekend. It was nearly twelve o'clock before his secretary came in to tell him that Mrs Gates was there with a gentleman and wanted to see him.

Puzzled, because she hardly ever came to the bank, he came out of his office to greet her and found her standing just inside the entrance with a man beside her whom Roger had never seen before. He was the kind of man whom it would be very easy to forget, even if he had met him. He was about thirty-five, but was going a little bald already, was of medium height and fairly bony and was wearing a rather shabby raincoat. He had a pale, very ordinary face; indeed there was an almost noticeable ordinariness about him, except for a slight grimness in his expression.

Coralie did not introduce him. She was looking shaken and shrinking. Roger had automatically held out his hand to the man, but he had appeared not to notice it.

'Well, come in,' Roger said and led the way back into his office, closing the door behind them.

Coralie dropped at once into a chair and though Roger asked the man to sit down, he ignored the invitation and remained standing. Roger went to the chair behind his desk.

'Well?' he said with all the cheeriness that he could force into his voice, just as if he believed that the man had come to open a big bank account. 'What can I do for you?'

'It's my fault,' Coralie said with a tremble in her voice. 'I told the gentleman who you were and persuaded him to come to see you instead of taking any other steps at once. It was kind of him to have come.'

'What does this mean?' Roger asked with sudden sternness in his voice. 'Who are you?'

'I'm the store detective at Jarvis and Jarvis,' the man answered in a flat voice, as if he were only too used to having to explain himself. Jarvis and Jarvis was the big supermarket a little way up the main street. 'And I'm sorry to have to tell you that I detected Mrs Gates appropriating certain articles when she left the store without paying for them. Naturally I didn't challenge her until she'd actually left the store, but once she was out in the street I spoke to her and she admitted she'd taken the things.'

'Good God, Coralie, what have you been up to?' Roger exclaimed. 'What things?'

'Just some tights and a bra,' she said. 'I told the gentleman who you were and that if he'd come here with me you'd pay for them. I really didn't know I hadn't paid for them, but it's quite true, they aren't on my receipt. I'm so terribly absent-minded nowadays, half the time I don't know what I'm doing.'

Roger felt his temper rising. In the intimate atmosphere of the village it had not been too difficult to keep it under control, to trust to the sympathy of the McQueens and to that of neigh-bours who knew Coralie's recent history. But here in the bank it was another matter.

'It's beginning to look as if you ought not to be out on your own,' he said harshly. He looked at the man. 'Of course I'll pay for the things, but will that be the end of the matter?'

'I can't really say,' the man replied in his toneless voice. 'I'll have to report the matter to the manager and it's up to the people at the top whether or not they call in the police and bring a charge.'

'A charge!' Roger said. 'In the magistrates' court? You mean they may actually do that?'

'They're entitled to do it. There was another witness to the event, so it wouldn't be difficult for them, and they've had a good deal of trouble of this sort lately. They may want to make an example.'

'But if I pay . . .'

'I'm afraid I can't accept payment, sir. The goods have been returned and in any case, it isn't up to me to decide. I merely observed the lady slip them into a bag she was carrying and then fail to produce them at the check-out counter.'

'But I thought all the stores were terrifically insured against shop-lifting,' Coralie said, 'so even if I'd done something so crazy they wouldn't have lost by it.'

'Coralie, please,' Roger said bitingly. 'Don't make things worse than they are.'

But how could anything be much worse than having the possibility hanging over him, as apparently he had, that his wife, the wife of the manager of the main bank in the town, might be charged with shop-lifting?

He spoke again to the man. 'I'm not trying to excuse her, but my wife has been seriously ill recently and literally doesn't know what she's doing sometimes. And we're moving away shortly, going to London. Perhaps that will affect the situation.'

'I'll certainly include it in my report,' the man said. 'How soon would that be?'

'Within a month at the longest.'

It would not be easy to arrange everything so soon, but if it had to be done to prevent the horror of the scandal here that Roger foresaw, it would have to be managed somehow. In London, where they were unknown, her strange behaviour, if it continued, could not be quite so disastrous. And for sure he would get her into the hands of a psychiatrist.

'Well, I'll do my best for you, sir,' the man said, 'and I dare say in the circumstances it may be no further steps will be taken.'

'There, didn't I say he was kind?' Coralie said with a sudden charming smile. 'Now I think I'll go home if they aren't going to arrest me.'

She stood up and left the office giving a little bow to the detective as she went.

For some time after the detective also had gone Roger sat staring before him, but it was not until the evening, shortly before his normal time for leaving the bank, that he wrote three letters. He did not dictate them to his secretary, but wrote them himself. One was accepting the appointment that he had been offered in London. One was resigning from his position in Allingford. One was to one of the larger house-agents in London. It was almost dark by the time that he reached home, but he felt a deep reluctance to go into the house to join Coralie.

When he had put his car away in the garage he strolled out into the garden and wandered up and down the paths.

The colours of the flowers were all lost in the dusk. The pale pink clematis was a shadowy white, the forsythia looked almost black, the daffodils seemed to have vanished. Perhaps it was as well, he thought. In any case he was going to have to give it all up, so he might as well accustom himself to the idea that the colours, the scents, the ever-changing patterns there that had so delighted him, had been prepared for someone else. Someone who would probably change everything, pull up what he had cherished, add what had no attraction for him.

Suddenly feeling extraordinarily tired, he at last went into the house.

Coralie was talking to someone. He heard her as soon as he opened the kitchen door. She was at the telephone in the hall. Still not quite ready to talk to her normally, or to discuss what had happened that morning, he stayed where he was.

He heard her say, 'But, darling, don't you understand, your idea, it's worked! I feel so excited. At first I didn't think it was going to. Those people in the village shop were so bloody kind-hearted that I believe I could have walked off with half their stock without their making a fuss. So today I took the risk of nicking a bra and some tights from the supermarket in town and made sure their detective saw me. But of course it might have meant getting involved with the police and being charged in court, which was a bit more than I was counting on . . . What? . . . Oh, he hasn't come home yet, it's quite all right, I can talk. And I managed to get the detective to go with me to see him, and the risk of the real scandal there'd be if the shop decided to prosecute scared him stiff and he told the man we were leaving for London in a few weeks. So everything's going to be fine. It'll be so easy to meet. Meanwhile I've seen no reason to tell him that the child wasn't his . . .'

It was at that point that Roger lost his head. Lunging across the kitchen, he seized her round the neck as she stood at the telephone and shook her and shook her until he knew that her neck was broken. She had replaced the receiver: there was no one to hear her screams. Then at last and somehow aimlessly he let her fall to the floor and stood looking down at her vacantly, as if he wondered what she was doing there.

It took him some minutes to decide what to do next. At last he moved her, but only to the bottom of the stairs, where he dropped her again, pulling her legs up on to the lower steps, spreading her arms out as if she had made a desperate attempt to save herself as she fell and arranging her with her face buried in the rug at the bottom. He thought it looked convincing. Then he telephoned Matthew Bayliss.

'Matthew, can you come round at once?' he asked. It did not matter that his voice was shaking, that was only natural. 'Coralie's had a terrible accident – tripped on the stairs – fallen – I'm afraid she's – as a matter of fact, I'm sure . . . She had a very nasty experience this morning and was very shaken. I oughtn't to have left her alone . . . Yes, yes, but please come.'

He put the telephone down, then he went into the sitting-room and threw the three letters that he had not yet posted into the fire. Was that what he had meant to do with them all along?

CHRISTINE GREEN

'Green's writing has all the requisite crackle and tension.'

Kate Saunders in the EVENING STANDARD

DRUMMOND
STREET

THE DAY the man from the Water Board went missing in Drummond Street was hot and humid. The washing on the lines hung still and dogs lay sleeping in the yards of the back-to-back houses. It was 'factory fortnight' and the local factories in Grindle had shut down for the annual holiday in late July.

Some of the younger people in Drummond Street had gone on holiday to Blackpool or Scarborough or even Majorca. The pensioners or the keen gardeners or those too poor to go on holiday had stayed at home.

Three people at the top end of the street had seen the Water Board man. He was warning them that the water would be off for two hours in the morning the following day.

He hadn't been seen again, not in Drummond Street or any other street. His wife reported him missing at six o'clock that evening.

'He'll have gone for a drink in the pub, a hot day like today,' said the desk sergeant at Grindle police station, trying to be reassuring and kind.

'He doesn't drink,' said the wife. And then she rang every hour on the hour until at 10 p.m. the Sergeant asked the CID to send someone along to see the wife as he couldn't spare a uniformed man.

Inspector Keith Lomloch agreed to go. He knew Drummond Street quite well and he was bored. Crime in factory fortnight had reached an all-time low. Even a missing Water Board man would break the tedium of an evening spent in a stuffy office.

The desk sergeant told him that a senior official from the

Water Board, Alan Wickersley, had been along to Drummond Street at about three and only three houses seemed to have been visited. Drummond Street had been his last visit of the day.

Lomloch walked the short distance towards Jubilee Road and the home of the missing man. It was dark now but the air was still and humid. From the front gardens of the houses the scent of roses and honeysuckle lingered as if trapped in the unmoving air. A few people watched as he walked by and they smiled at him as they interrupted their neighbourly chats about the good weather and how on such a day they would have liked to feel a sea breeze. Occasionally he heard the clink of milk bottles being put on steps, the cry of a fractious child, televisions seeming louder than usual because windows were wide open. At number twenty-one he stopped. A woman had opened the curtains. She had been waiting for him. Lomloch suddenly wished he could just keep on walking.

The wife, whose name was Gillian, was anxious, but adamant that disaster had befallen her husband.

'We've been married sixteen years. He's never been late before.'

'Never?' asked Lomloch. He was always late.

'Never,' repeated Mrs Wickersley firmly.

'You hadn't had a row or anything?'

Gillian Wickersley fixed him with a baleful glare. 'You sit down, Inspector,' she said. 'Your men are out looking for him aren't they?'

'Of course they are,' he lied. Missing adult persons usually rated only one visit from a uniformed constable and after that the case would be off-loaded to the Salvation Army.

He sat down on a well-worn armchair and watched Gillian Wickersley. She was, he supposed, about thirty-five, the sort of age that in women's magazines was portrayed as being glamorous and dynamic. In Grindle, a woman of thirty-five was neither – they were 'getting on'. Gillian had streaks of grey in her hair, her body was thin and formless and around her reddened eyes lines had etched themselves in, as though little creatures had burrowed there. Lomloch considered himself a good judge of women. She had probably been pretty, once.

'Tell me about your husband,' he said.

Her hands nervously smoothed the material of the flowered apron she wore. 'What do you want to know?' she asked, looking up swiftly in irritation.

'Now come on love,' said Lomloch, 'I'm trying to help. Tell me what he's like.'

'Like?' she echoed. 'Well he's – he's just ordinary. Not very tall, fair crinkly sort of hair, blue eyes.'

'Any enemies?'

'He works for the Water Board,' she said incredulously.

'Drink? Gambling? Women? Drugs? Men?' queried Lomloch getting just about every vice out of the way.

Mrs Wickersley was stunned into painful silence. 'Look here, Inspector,' she said eventually. 'We're just ordinary folk. We've got two kids. My husband's only interests are his family and football. We go out together every Saturday night, my mum stays with the children, and usually we go to the sports club. We're just ordinary.'

'And your husband wasn't depressed or worried about money?'

'We're not in debt, if that's what you mean. We don't run a car and the house is nearly paid for. And I'm careful with money. We manage very well.'

Lomloch was beginning to feel he wasn't just barking up the wrong tree, he was in an entirely different forest.

'Is there anyone he could have decided to visit?'

'Not without telling me. He'd promised to take Jason to the park tonight to play cricket. He always keeps his promises.' Her voice broke and tears welled in her eyes.

'I've rung the local hospitals,' she said. 'I've rung everybody I could think of.'

Lomloch felt awkward. He murmured something about grown men not disappearing unless they wanted to. And then was ashamed of himself when she began crying in earnest. He had definitely said the wrong thing.

'Now then Mrs Wickersley, stop crying,' he blustered, as he stood up and patted her on the shoulder. 'We'll find him, I promise you that. There's probably a very simple explanation.'

She sniffed, grabbed a tissue from a box on the arm of the sofa and said, 'Which is?'

'What I mean is – well . . .' Lomloch trailed off. 'I've said we'll find him and we will.'

With a hand to her mouth, as though trying to stifle more tears, she nodded.

Lomloch promised to return as soon as he had any news. He urged her to get some rest and asked if she'd like her mother informed.

'Not yet,' she said. 'Not yet.'

He took with him a recent photograph. A smiling man, slightly built, the sort of face that stays boyish.

As Lomloch walked the short distance to Drummond Street he sensed that this wasn't going to be an easy case. Idly he went over the possibilities in his mind. Alan, bored with Saturday nights in the sports club and his dull but worthy wife, had done the proverbial 'runner'. Or he had succumbed to the charms of a bored but sexy housewife and had fallen asleep in her scented arms after a few stolen hours of passion. Or maybe he had a head injury and was wandering around Grindle with loss of memory. Perhaps little green men from Mars had landed on a bit of waste-ground and the only humanoid specimen they could find in the holiday fortnight was poor old Alan. Or he could be dead. Murdered even.

All was quiet in Drummond Street. One streetlamp lit the alley between the backs of the two-up two-down terraced houses. On the worn cobbles a cat lay sleeping by a gate. Alan Wickersley's last calls of the day had been here, according to both his wife and his employers. The cat barred the way to the first back gate. Lomloch watched the cat for a moment.

'Did you see him, puss?' he asked. The cat, sensing someone was there, woke and rubbed his head against Lomloch's trousers. Then he settled happily on his shoe. Lomloch moved the cat from his foot and lifted the latch of the back gate of the first house. He knocked firmly on the door, too firmly. The piercing screams of a baby rent the still of the night. When the door finally opened it was swung open as if in a fury and a young woman stood there with an angry expression and a 'you bastard' on her lips. Lomloch guessed she was about eighteen, her cheeks still childlike, soft and rounded but with adult dark rings under her brown eyes.

'I thought you were someone else,' she said. 'What the hell do you want at this time of night? You've just woken the baby, poor little bugger's teething.'

'Police.'

'Oh,' she said, not in the least surprised. 'What's he been up to this time?'

There was a momentary pause in the child's screaming but it soon resumed more loudly, more persistently. He or she had simply paused for breath. Lomloch raised his voice to be heard over the noise.

'Nothing that I know of – yet. Unless, that is, he's had something to do with a missing person.'

She smiled, relieved. 'Come on in then. If it was a missing car radio or a video that might be him, but he hasn't gone in for kidnapping yet. I mean he couldn't come home and tell me a person had fallen off the back of a lorry, could he?'

As Lomloch stepped into the kitchen the warmth hit him. The room felt stifling. A cigarette lay burning in an ash-tray, a romantic novel open on the table. In the air a smell lingered; he recognised it, the smell of wet nappies and baby powder. Strangely it wasn't unpleasant. He sat down at the table as the young woman went upstairs to the baby. The child quietened after a minute or two. Lomloch flicked the book over. The hero was speaking through gritted teeth, the heroine was biting her lips and trying to control her 'fast-beating heart' and the 'uncontrollable waves of desire that swept through her'. The hero was saying hoarsely: 'My darling, my darling, if only, if only . . .' Lomloch was just about to turn the page to find the answer to the 'if only' riddle when the young mother returned with her baby in her arms.

The baby, large with tubularly fat legs had the bright red spots on his cheeks that Lomloch recognised as evidence of teething. The child was sighing now with exhaustion, strands of black hair plastered to its head with sweat, beads of moisture on the forehead.

'Boy or girl?' he asked. The child began to wriggle in agitation, the nappy sagging and obviously wet.

'She's Tammy. She's fifteen months, she's nearly walking. She's ever so hot, you don't think she's got a bug or anything, do you? I mean she could be ill couldn't she? She's been whingeing all day.'

'She's a lovely baby. I should think it's just the heat. Or perhaps she's thirsty.'

'Yeah,' said the girl. 'I'll give her some juice.'

Lomloch watched as the baby gulped on a bottle of cherry-coloured liquid. He liked babies. They were uncomplicated, they didn't cheat, lie or murder. And a baby's smile could lift the heaviest heart.

The young mother's name was Samantha, Sam for short. She lived with Darren, on and off, and lately it had been more off than on. Lomloch told her about the missing man from the Water Board.

'Yeah. I saw him,' said Sam. The baby gulped the last few drops from the bottle and then closed her eyes in a sort of exhausted ecstasy.

'He was a nice bloke. I hadn't seen him around here before.'

'Did he say where he was going next?'

'He said he was doing all the houses in the street. Warning about the cut off.'

'Did you see where he went when he left?'

Sam shook her black pony-tail. 'No. Tammy was whingeing and I tried putting her in her push-chair and rocking her. You know, backwards and forwards. Dead boring but sometimes it works.'

Lomloch nodded. 'Thanks for your help, Sam.'

'That's all right,' said Sam. 'Shame he's missing. I was reading my horoscope when he came. We had a little chat about that. He said his horoscope was good for the day. It said "Good luck will come your way like a bolt from the blue." You can't believe these things can you?'

'Have to take horoscopes with a pinch of salt,' said Lomloch.

'You got kids?' asked Sam.

Lomloch shook his head.

'It's all right for men,' said Sam as she wiped the baby's forehead with a tissue. 'They do all the playing and get all the gurgles and smiles and then at three in the morning they tell you it's *your* kid that's screaming. Did the missing bloke have kids?'

'Two.'

'There you are then. Hot day, hot night. Perhaps he'd just had enough. He's gone off somewhere, like Darren does when the crying gets him down. Perhaps he's gone to the seaside. I haven't seen the sea in years. I did go once to Blackpool for a whole week. It was great. It only rained twice. One day I'll go again, when Tammy's old enough for a bucket and spade.'

When Lomloch left Tammy was asleep in Sam's arms, the wet nappy still in place. As he closed the back door Sam had sat down and resumed her reading. Romance between the covers of a book was the most a young mother could expect in Grindle, and that thought depressed Lomloch. He could have sunk two pints easily. That was *his* escape.

The back gate of the next house was painted a dull green, or at least it had been painted once. Long ago. Now the wood was exposed and the paint had shrivelled in places, and he had to lift the gate to open it; and even then it was so mishung and warped that it grated open rather than swung. He had to knock the back door and call 'Police' three times before it finally opened.

An elderly lady, white hair covered by a hair-net and wearing a red quilted dressing-gown said: 'Yes, pet. What is it?'

'I'm Police Inspector Lomloch. I'm trying to trace a missing Water Board official. Drummond Street was his last call of the day and as yet he hasn't returned home.'

'You'd better come in. Have you got your warrant card?'

Lomloch smiled. 'Good for you, Mrs . . . ?' he said as he showed her his identification.

'Mrs Armsby I am, and you can't be too careful these days, can you?'

Lomloch followed her into a tiny back room that smelt of stewed lamb and cabbage and had a budgie on a stand in one corner.

'Sit down, pet. Would you like a cup of tea?'

Lomloch declined. He was a lager man.

'Did you see the Water Board man this afternoon, Mrs Armsby?'

'I did indeed,' she said as she sat down on the upright armchair opposite his. 'Nice young man. He had a glass of pop while he was here. He came to tell me the water was going off in the morning and I should make sure to fill a kettle.'

'Did he come in the house?'

She shook her head. 'I was sitting out in the garden for a few minutes. I brought his drink out to him.'

'I see,' said Lomloch feeling dispirited and not really knowing what else to ask.

'We had a nice chat,' she continued, 'he said he was taking his little son to the park in the evening to play cricket. He said he hoped it would be cooler by then.'

'What time was this?'

'About threeish I think. I'd long since had some dinner and a cup of tea and I was sitting in the garden resting my legs, ever so painful they get in hot weather.'

'So he seemed perfectly normal?'

'Oh yes. As I said, he was a nice young man. Such a shame he's missing. His poor wife and children. No one's safe these days are they, even grown men.'

'You didn't see anything unusual? Anyone strange hanging about?'

'Well, no, pet. Once that back gate's closed I don't go out again. I do my shopping in the morning and then that's it. I don't venture out again.'

'And you didn't hear anything?'

Mrs Armsby started to shake her head but then she said, 'All I heard was Ronald Brace. "Leeky" they call him. He shouts at the kids as they come up and down the alley on their bikes. I heard him shout once, otherwise it was quieter than usual.'

'Where does Mr Brace live?'

'Next door but one on the other side. Nice man, a retired miner. Grows leeks. Bachelor he is. Never married. Just as well because he doesn't like kids much. Still, if he's poorly I keep an eye on him. Us old ones have to look after each other, don't we?'

Lomloch nodded in agreement and thanked her.

'I do hope you find him,' she said, 'and call again any time. I don't see many people. It's always nice to have visitors.'

The next house was in darkness and there was no reply to his insistent knocking. Either they were still out or on holiday, and he realised he should have asked Mrs Armsby who in the street was away. Still, it was slightly better than being in a stuffy office, he consoled himself as he continued up Drummond Street.

Only a few houses were occupied and no one had seen Alan Wickersley. Lomloch had been to the top of the alley and now came down the other side. It would have been more sensible to criss-cross but it was growing cooler now and he didn't mind prolonging his search. He was off duty at midnight.

Mr Ronald Brace was in his back yard when Lomloch opened the gate. He looked up startled. He was grey haired and balding with his shirt-sleeves rolled up to his elbow, but his arms looked strong and his shoulders were broad. In front of him was a wheelbarrow full of gardening tools and by the side of the barrow two tin watering-cans.

Lomloch introduced himself and explained his mission.

'Missing you say,' said Brace. 'I haven't seen no Water Board man. Well, only the one that came this evening.'

'You're sure?' persisted Lomloch.

'Aye.'

'Did you see anyone about three this afternoon?'

'Only kids.'

'Were you in the whole afternoon, Mr Brace?'

Brace paused for a moment resting a hand on his wheelbarrow.

'I went to my allotment about four. Collected my tools. I allus do that. Kids get into my shed and pinch them.'

'I hear you grow leeks,' said Lomloch.

'You hear right,' said Brace. 'I've won the Grindle leek-growing competition three years in a row. Champion, my leeks are. Champion.'

Lomloch stood awkwardly for a moment saying nothing. The little green men from Mars were beginning to look like a real possibility . . .

'I can't stand around here,' said Brace. 'Water's off in the morning. I've got to fill me watering-cans and water the leeks.'

'Now?'

'Aye. When it's cool is the best time. I allus do it late. A couple of nights before the showing I sleep in my shed. Just in case the kids come and steal my leeks. I've been right busy in my allotment just lately. Competition's real stiff this year. The younger ones are getting keen as mustard. Mind you I'm the one with the experience and the knowledge. I look after my leeks like babies. Just like babies.'

'Do the local kids give you much trouble?' asked Lomloch, aware that now they had a 'Community' policeman he could be asked to keep an eye on the allotments.

'Nothing I can't handle,' answered Brace. 'Only one little bastard gave me any trouble. Fair-haired kid in a blue tracksuit. Got a face like a ferret.'

Lomloch smiled. 'I'll be off then. Good luck with the leeks.'

The Brace house was the last, or at least the last to have an occupant. Lomloch felt a wave of disappointment. He would have to tell Gillian Wickersley the bad news, but carefully. He must neither be too pessimistic nor too optimistic. Men had gone missing before. Out to buy a packet of cigarettes never to return. The British police forces had never managed to find Lord Lucan yet alone a lowly Water Board man.

Back at the Police Station Lomloch was informed by the desk sergeant that Mrs Wickersley had rung again and was getting more frantic.

Lomloch went to his office, poured himself a can of lager and listened as Grindle's town hall clock struck the hour. It was midnight. Midnight! It hadn't taken him long to walk from Drummond to the station. Surely no one waters their leeks at nearly midnight, not even someone as obsessed with leeks as Ronald Brace. There's nowt as queer as folk, Lomloch told himself, but that didn't quell his doubts. Not suspicious by nature, he had, over the years, made a conscious effort to be more suspicious and less trusting. Where a doubt or a niggle existed in his mind it had to be exorcised. There was one other thing that troubled Lomloch. Brace had used the past tense when he talked about the boy. 'Only one little bastard *gave* me any trouble.' What did that mean? Was it significant? There was only one way to find out.

At the allotment Brace sat in the darkness outside his shed on a stool. The leeks growing in the patch in front of him glistened with droplets of water, their tall leaves proud and strong.

'Champion,' muttered Brace.

'Magnificent,' said Lomloch as he walked up and stood beside him.

'They're a miracle,' said Brace. 'When I was working it was growing leeks that kept me sane. Planning and reading and getting tips from other growers. I allus wanted to be a farmer you know. Out in the fresh air every day. Not spend half my life in a dark hell.'

'About the Water Board man . . .'

'Aye,' said Brace staring sadly at Lomloch for a few moments, and as he did so his eyes began to glisten like the water droplets on the leeks. 'He's here.'

'What happened?'

'It was that kid's fault. He used to come up here shouting and jeering. Said he'd get my leeks. Sometimes he'd bring his friends and I'd chase them off. "We'll be back, you stupid old sod," they'd shout. If there was no one else working the allotments I'd have to stay all day in the growing season. And all night. You get too old for all that worry, you know. I complained to his mum of course, but she said he didn't mean no harm and he was a good boy really. But he was always there watching me if you know what I mean . . .'

'And the Water Board man?'

'I was in my back yard, see, and the gate opened. I keep it locked because of him, a bolt at the top. This hand comes over and slides back the bolt. Then I saw the fair hair and a flash of blue and I thought, It's him the little so and so, and I had a hammer in my hand, I'd been fixing the fence, and I whacked him over the head just the once as his head came through the gate. Had to protect my babies, you see. But when I looked at him properly I knew it wasn't him. It wasn't the boy. I dragged him into the kitchen and then I had to wait until it was dark to bring him here in the wheelbarrow.'

'What were you going to do with him?' asked Lomloch. His stomach had begun to churn already at the thought of telling Mrs Wickersley.

'Keep him in the shed for a bit, I thought, and then after the leek show I could have buried him. Mind you it would have ruined next year's leeks.' He paused, looking out towards his crop. 'How did you know it was me?'

'I didn't. Not really. I just thought the late watering was a bit suspicious. And I wondered if you were using a hosepipe and that's illegal in a drought. I thought perhaps you and the Water Board hadn't seen eye to eye about that. Maybe a row had ensued. A fatal row.'

Brace didn't say anything for a moment.

'I'll go to prison, won't I?'

Lomloch nodded.

'Will I get bail?'

'You might.'

'I could still make the show then?'

Lomloch didn't answer.

'You'd better open the shed now, Mr Brace.'

Alan Wickersley sat propped against the shed's wooden side. Lomloch shone his torch on to the face. Blood had dribbled from his head down the side of his cheek. He still looked young. Only a few grey hairs glinted at his temples. His royal blue Water Board uniform was hardly creased.

Lomloch sighed deeply before using his radio.

After Brace's arrest he called at Jubilee Road to break the news to Gillian Wickersley. He stood on the doorstep, his hand raised and stilled, momentarily trying to work out exactly what he was going to say.

She knew immediately he had bad news. Lomloch didn't go into details. That could wait until the morning. He simply told her Alan was dead with a head injury. Although she paled and sat with her head in her hands, she didn't cry.

'I knew he hadn't deserted me,' she said. 'I knew he'd come home if he could.'

Lomloch asked if he could ring anyone to sit with her. She refused.

'I'll be all right,' she said. 'My Paul's out looking for his Dad. I told him not to be long.'

'Paul?' queried Lomloch.

'My eldest. He's fifteen. We had a big gap between him and Jason. Jason's only six.'

'I'll wait till he comes home,' said Lomloch.

They sat in silence for a while. Gillian stared at the blank television screen. Staring, as though she was viewing in her imagination either her past life or some lonely scary future.

Their eyes turned to the door when they heard the click-click of bike wheels. The front door opened and closed and then the living-room door opened just slightly. A head appeared. Fair crinkly sort of hair, a face like a ferret.

'I couldn't find him Mum,' he said. 'I'm going to bed.' And, in a flash of blue, he was gone.

BILL JAMES

'Mr James is bruisingly good and deserves
to win converts.'

Sunday Telegraph

FOR INFORMATION
ONLY

As to grassing, it's not a career you would recommend to your children. No, not quite mainstream, yet surely of importance. You could even say crucial. In any case, few grasses, including this one, have children. The life's too what might be called up and down, meaning full of peril.

There's a murder now in these parts where some grassing – i.e., secretly slipping information to detectives – will be very much to the point, but even if this was generally known, which pray God it won't be, the skills would get no recognition. Obviously, grassing has what is sometimes referred to as a stigma, and even the ones you grass to, and whose front-page glories you create – that is, the police – despise you the same as everyone else. They have a truck load of grubby names for those taking mighty risks in their interests: terms such as 'touts', 'snouts', 'narks', 'earholes', 'whisperers', and, of course 'grasses' – these last two being more or less the same, as a matter of fact, taken from 'whispering grass'.

This particular murder is like a lot of others, a villain exterminated by a villain, or villains. It is the kind of hellish crime where police run into what is always described in the tabloids as a wall of silence: nobody will talk to them, not even the friends and relatives of the corpse. You see, co-operation with police is something they have not been nurtured to, and no matter what happens, they cannot change their habits. Now, this is where the grass comes in. He will usually be on what is referred to as the inside – which clearly does not mean 'inside', as we sometimes refer to those doing a jail sentence, but on the inside of the communities concerned. As such, he might hear matters police never would. This boy can enter a club or pub without causing all conversation immediate cardiac arrest, which is what happens when plain-clothes police slink in, posing as humans. This murder is very messy and sick, as so many of them are when it's heavy against heavy, or heavies: singular or plural is one of the matters I'm not too sure about at this moment in time, but I'm working on it.

Now, the obvious question is, if most of the people in these communities will not open their mouths to police, why does the grass, he being also a member of a community? Why does he defy the local culture? This is some poser, and, to be frank, it's where treachery comes in. Your true grass is a loner, but a loner pretending to be one of the band. A guise is what this is sometimes referred to as. It is not easy to keep up. After a few unexplainable arrests, some in the community may suspect or half suspect a certain grass is, well, a grass. But as long as they don't know it for sure and totally, the grass is usually safe. Safeish. It's an uncertain kind of career, though, there's no denying it – not at all like working in local government – which is why at this stage I would not think of marriage or a family.

To answer the question, then – why does a grass grass? – let's approach it from the side: a grass – this is to say, a decent-quality, experienced grass – is selective. He does not blab, blab, blab about every bit of criminality he knows of. He makes what could be termed a moral judgment. Example: he might not say a word anywhere about a burglary where nobody is hurt, and where insurance will take care of all losses, anyway. This is even if the takings run into hundreds of grand. A grass is not like some priest or Bible puncher, pursuing an all-out holy campaign against every sin. His and theirs are quite different professions, though all worthwhile. As a matter of fact, I prefer the name, 'informant', to 'grass', and to any of those other crude pieces of slang, informant having a weighty, rather civic sound.

But take this murder. The location is a children's playground in a public park, which gives a rather gross tinge from the start. Surely, there are some pieces of territory which should never be involved in crimes of violence and where everything to do with a murder is totally inappropriate. Think, for instance, of the gardens of a convent containing the pious, or the surrounds of a gallery which is filled with wonderful and timeless paintings – eminent names like Velasquez. Or think of this innocent children's playground. Yet, the fact is, here you have a Number Two or Three in one of the local drug, pimping and protection outfits pinned to the soil by a metal stake through the mouth and coming out at the back of his neck and into the earth to a depth of a full nine inches, unarguably sledgehammer work. That is my information – held back by the authorities from the Press and broadcasters because of its acute unpleasantness, but discoverable to those like self, for whom it is, if such a phrase is permissible in the circumstances, bread and butter.

Now, this is the sort of death nobody needs. This is the sort of death that would be out of order enough in the middle of a remote field or on the mud flats, but when it comes to Cedric Lyndon Chivers he is discovered naked alongside that harmless chunky green-and-red-wood climbing-frame of the play area, and not so very far from the very smallest slide, meant for dear little toddlers.

My understanding is that, despite a gunshot wound in the chest, the forensic people say he was alive when that stake was forced into his mouth and thumped through. (The point about grasses – at least, about those of a certain stature – is that information moves two ways: mostly *towards* the police, of course, but this and that *from* the police, as well.) These findings could mean he was shot and disabled somewhere else, then brought here and throat-pinned in that barbaric fashion, copied, as I've heard, from the Vikings, who were famously short of what is known as compunction. Imagine the kind of mind or minds that would make a special effort to give Cedric this display in such a normally carefree setting.

This is my point about selectivity. Who's going to tell me that the perpetrator or perpetrators of the outrage should be allowed to hide behind a so-called wall of silence? I ask you, who? This is culture? Certainly not culture a chairman of the Arts Council would appreciate, or the late Dame Margot

Fonteyn. Does anyone comprehend how those close to Cedric – business colleagues, as it were, or parents, who live locally – could keep quiet about what they know or suspect? With glossy first names like these – Cedric Lyndon – it is clear that the parents had bright hopes for their child. They certainly did not visualise this kind of unsightly end. Yet my information is that they will say nothing about his last known movements, nor about special enemies. To the Press, they commented that they had no idea who could have done such a thing to their beloved boy, because he was so all-round popular and good-hearted, with a life-long interest in the breeding of Sealyhams, those piss-everywhere white dogs with a big head and very short legs.

Grassing – you will be beginning to see – has its virtues, in fact has its indispensable side, even if it will never bring a knighthood. Grassing in this kind of situation is a discreet public service. Surely it is reasonable to open one's mouth if another mouth has been prised open and a lump of steel rammed through it. Of course, I am not saying that Cedric's friends and relatives believe the murder should be accepted and forgotten about, and that this is why they make no disclosures. Here, again, we have a major point to do with grassing. Those who worked with and/or were even fond of Cedric – not easy, because he was a towering shit-heap – those linked to him, I say, one way or the other, regardless, will look for means to put things right, as their evasive lingo goes. That's to say, vengeance. One reason they tell the police nothing is because these people want to deal with the problem themselves. This is referred to also as sorting it out.

Which suggests a kind of warfare – the gang kind. Society at large wants that? I take leave to think not. In war, all sorts can be hurt, not just the participants. You might get bullets on the busy streets, fast, murderous cars, even explosions. Is anyone going to tell me that there is no duty to prevent this happening, if at all possible? Who can do it but the grass? Obviously, police have a rough idea of who's in the gangs and how they operate and who might have been stalking Cedric. Rough ideas and might have been are no use to the courts, though. And they don't tell you where the next outbreak of blood-stained trouble might come. These, again, are matters that the grass can often assist with very materially.

A further important point is that revenge can be merely approximate. People get hit, yes, but are they the right people? What revenge is often referred to in books of quotations and so on as is 'a kind of wild justice', which comes from some top-class thinker. Notice that 'wild'. This is not a controlled, proved matter. This is instinct stoked up with hate, obviously involving a big danger of mistakes. This is hardly the venerated jury system, with its 'If you please, my Lord', plus wigs and innocent until proved guilty. But the grass can introduce that other element, the exactness, the rightness, the facts – well, the justice. Isn't his a vital role? (By the way, women don't seem to take to it much.)

Police will know, naturally, that this showpiece deterrent death is something to do with mishandling of drugs or profits by the late Cedric Lyndon, probably coke, maybe crack. It could be over-mixing stuff with filler, or selling higher than is accounted for and holding back a juicy personal take, or even using some of the merchandise himself, then starting to mind-float and getting careless, and maybe doing some silly talking or, possibly, losing part of the consignment in a club or slag's room. This is the sort of important detail that can come a grass's way if the grass is on what is known as the *qui vive* and is fairly well trusted all round.

I will not hide the fact that one's own activities may, of course, benefit as a result of successful grassing. The rather coarse saying, 'You scratch my back and I'll scratch yours', does have a bearing. Grassing is not entirely a selfless public service like the Samaritans. This mutual relationship need not always mean the passing of money from the police, but there can be a certain useful absence of pressure, instead. Example: there is an art dealer called Jack Lamb not far from here, generally thought to be a top-flight informant, and he goes from strength to strength, even though some of the works he buys and sells on the quiet could come from anywhere, meaning deeply illegal. Yes, what is known in the art game as provenance

– signifying how the painting was got and where from – is assuredly not one of Jack's strongest sides. But, on account of grassing, he has other assets, such as the cop he talks to, who offers a certain powerful influence on Jack's behalf. Myself, I do a little commerce in various commodities, at a much lower level than Jack Lamb, obviously, but I admit there is sometimes a doubt or two over by what means certain items I have for sale originally came on to the open market. All right, maybe from theft. But, within reason, curiosity relating to these is not pressed by detectives. They are responding to my established ability to put helpful matter their way – often referred to in the eventual successful trials within the police-witness phrase 'acting on information received'. Hence my preference for the term informant.

Harpur said: 'Francis Garland has a small-time but sometimes reliable grass, sir, who's now reporting that Cedric was done by Gordon Hamm and Antichrist Jessop – sorry, Jeremy Lisle Vincent Jessop.'

'I want someone else for that? Don't we want someone else for that, Colin? Can we shut the bugger up?' Iles replied.

'Which bugger?'

'What?'

'Well, the grass or Francis, sir?'

The Assistant Chief Constable, who was bent forward over the desk examining some blemish on his wrist, nodded his fine grey head to acknowledge a fair point. 'I meant the grass. But you could be right. Garland's the very model of a thrusting detective chief inspector and naturally wants his discoveries given due weight.'

'Especially when they could be true, sir.'

Iles held his hand under the direct beam of the table lamp and stared harder. 'Nothing genito-urinary first shows itself on the wrist, does it, Colin? Of course, you'll know that pox need not be just a simple trousers job.'

'I can probably explain our tactics convincingly to Francis.'

'Yes, do: explain them to him very convincingly, Col. We

have someone else well and truly in the frame for Cedric, and don't want to be messing about with nobodies. Not at this stage. Can we take the grass in, to keep him quiet? Presumably we've been going easy on some of his own shady work as quid pro quo? We could stop blind-eyeing and get him celled? That would be one answer.'

'Well, it's much against the spirit, sir. The grassing code.'

Iles raised his head and smiled. It was that saintly smile he sometimes graced the world with, a different species altogether from his more usual Herod smile. 'True, Colin. Commitments. Grasses are rubbish, but they're *our* rubbish.'

'This grass talks exclusively to Garland, sir, so perhaps there is no real danger of word about Hamm and Antichrist getting out.'

'He talks exclusively to Garland as long as he sees some response. But if not? He's got information to sell. The Press?'

'The Press can't risk libelling Gordon Hamm and Antichrist just on the say-so of a grass, sir. Jessop's got social status. He wears hand-made suits.'

'Jerk,' Iles replied. 'No wonder you're stuck at Chief Superintendent. Newspapers could still unleash their bloody specialist investigative people. They think they can find their way round libel, and often can. Look, I want Martin Gabalfa for Cedric Chivers' death, not a couple of hacks like Gordon Hamm and Jessop. And Martin did quite possibly give the orders for it. Press people, digging away, crowding, interviewing – they could very soon fuck up the whole thing with red herrings.'

'Meaning with what might be true, sir?'

'Colin, what's true—'

'Is what a jury believes.'

'Is *still* what a jury believes – even after the Birmingham Six. We've built a sweet and almost full case against Gabalfa, yes?'

'Not bad.'

'All right, perhaps he didn't personally do it, but will we ever nail him for the foul things he does personally do?'

'Probably not, sir.'

'Including deaths?'

'Including deaths.'

'Perhaps not this specific death, but enough others. Many others?'

'Almost certainly.'

'I like your modest way with words, Harpur, you snivelling, quibbling also-ran. So, Col, if this is looked at intelligently, dispassionately, I'd say take the grass in for a while on something fairly minor, but definitely not bailable. Or even hint we'd leak a rumour to Gordon and Antichrist that he's shopping them. That should keep him quiet. We can do Gordon and Antichrist for something else when convenient. This is clean-sweep, strategic thinking – the long term. It's what's expected when you reach my rank Col, which you never will, of course.'

'Well, I might be able to manage this business some other, less painful way, sir. I'll get Garland to let me see the grass and have a chat. It might take a few days to persuade Francis, though.'

'Manage it how you like. Manage it.'

What's known as sacrosanct, almost holy, is the relationship between a grass and his cop contact. This is totally private, one-to-one, what is sometimes also referred to as symbiotic, meaning they depend on each other. So I was more than surprised, you could say enraged, to see my police contact, namely Detective Chief Inspector Francis Garland, turning up to a secret rendezvous in certain disused railway carriages on a siding with another cop accompanying – viz., his boss, Detective Chief Superintendent Colin Harpur. This one was known to all, and, as police go, is straight in many ways, but also sharp and hard and, anyway, constantly leaned on to bend rules by that real piece of evil and merrymaking they've got down there, ACC Desmond Iles, i/c Operations – without anaesthetic.

'Well, I've heard with admiration of your work,' Harpur said. 'You're totally anonymous to me, of course. Francis wouldn't ever reveal an identity. But the outline of your career is impressive and it's a golden comfort to us desk-based creatures that we have someone in the field like yourself.'

The word 'golden' I like a lot. It always sets up a promising

IAN RANKIN

'Rankin's ability to create a credible character, delivering convincing dialogue to complement sinister and hardhitting plots set against vividly detailed atmosphere, is awesome.'

TIME OUT

IN THE FRAME

INSPECTOR John Rebus placed the letters on his desk.

There were three of them. Small, plain white envelopes, locally franked, the same name and address printed on each in a careful hand. The name was K. Leighton. Rebus looked up from the envelopes to the man sitting on the other side of the desk. He was in his forties, frail-looking and restless. He had started talking the moment he'd entered Rebus's office, and didn't seem inclined to stop.

'The first one arrived on Tuesday, last Tuesday. A crank, I thought, some sort of malicious joke. Not that I could think of anyone who might do that sort of thing.' He shifted in his seat. 'My neighbours over the back from me . . . well, we don't always see eye to eye, but they wouldn't resort to this.' His eyes glanced up towards Rebus for a second. 'Would they?'

'You tell me, Mr Leighton.'

As soon as he'd said this, Rebus regretted the choice of words. Undoubtedly, Kenneth Leighton *would* tell him. Rebus opened the first envelope's flap, extracted the sheet of writing-paper and unfolded it. He did the same with the second and third letters and laid all three before him.

'If it had been only the one,' Kenneth Leighton was saying, 'I wouldn't have minded, but it doesn't look as though they're going to stop. Tuesday, then Thursday, then Saturday. I spent all weekend worrying about what to do . . .'

'You did the right thing, Mr Leighton.'

Leighton wriggled pleasurably. 'Well, they always say you should go to the police. Not that I think there's anything serious. I mean, *I've* not got anything to hide. My life's an open book . . .'

123

An open book and an unexciting one, Rebus would imagine. He tried to shut out Leighton's voice and concentrated instead on the first letter.

> Mr Leighton,
> We've got photos you wouldn't want your
> wife to see, believe us. Think about it.
> We'll be in touch.

Then the second:

> Mr Leighton,
> £2,000 for the photos. That seems fair,
> doesn't it? You really wouldn't want
> your wife to see them. Get the money.
> We'll be in touch.

And the third:

> Mr Leighton,
> We'll be sending one reprint to show we
> mean business. You'd better get to it
> before your wife does. There are plenty
> more copies.

Rebus looked up, and caught Leighton staring at him. Leighton immediately looked away. Rebus had the feeling that if he stood behind the man and said 'boo' quite softly in his ear, Leighton would melt all down the chair. He looked like the sort of person who might make an enemy of his neighbours, complaining too strenuously about a noisy party or a family row. He looked like a crank.

'You haven't received the photo yet?'

Leighton shook his head. 'I'd have brought it along, wouldn't I?'

'And you've no idea what sort of photo it might be?'

'None at all. The last time somebody took my picture was at my niece's wedding.'

'And when was that?'

'Three years ago. You see what I'm saying, Inspector? This doesn't make any sense.'

'It must make sense to at least one person, Mr Leighton.' Rebus nodded towards the letters.

They had been written in blue ball-point, the same pen which had been used to address the envelopes. A cheap blue ball-point, leaving smears and blots of ink. It was anything but professional-looking. The whole thing looked like a joke. Since when did blackmailers use their own handwriting? Anyone with a rudimentary education in films, TV cop shows and thriller novels knew that you used a typewriter or letters cut out of newspapers, or whatever; anything that would produce a dramatic effect. These letters were too personal to look dramatic. Polite, too: that use of 'Mr Leighton' at the start of each one. A particular word caught Rebus's attention and held it. But then Leighton said something interesting.

'I don't even have a wife, not now.'

'You're not married?'

'I was. Divorced six years ago. Six years and one month.'

'And where's your wife now, Mr Leighton?'

'Remarried, lives in Glenrothes. I got an invite to the wedding, but I didn't go. Can't remember what I sent them for a present . . .' Leighton was lost in thought for a moment, then collected himself. 'So you see, if these letters are written by someone I know, how come they *don't* know I'm divorced?'

It was a good question. Rebus considered it for a full five seconds. Then he came to his conclusion.

'Let's leave it for now, Mr Leighton,' he said. 'There's not much we can do till this photo arrives . . . *if* it arrives.'

Leighton looked numb, watching Rebus fold the letters and replace them in their envelopes. Rebus wasn't sure what the man had expected. Fingerprints lifted from the envelopes by forensic experts? A tell-tale fibre leading to an arrest? Handwriting identified . . . saliva from the stamps and the envelope-flaps checked . . . psychologists analysing the wording of the messages themselves, coming up with a profile of the blackmailer? It was all good stuff, but not on a wet Monday morning in Edinburgh. Not with CID's case-load and budget restrictions.

'Is that it?'

Rebus shrugged. That was it. We're only human, Mr Leighton. For a moment, Rebus thought he'd actually voiced his thoughts. He had not. Leighton still sat there, pale and disappointed, his mouth set like the bottom line of a balance sheet.

'Sorry,' said Rebus, rising.

'I've just remembered,' said Leighton.

'What?'

'Six wine glasses, that's what I gave them. Caithness glass they were too.'

'Very nice I'm sure,' said Rebus, stifling a post-weekend yawn as he opened the office door.

But Rebus was certainly intrigued.

No wife these past six years, and the last photograph of Leighton dated back three years to a family wedding. Where was the material for a blackmail? Where the motive? Means, motive and opportunity. Means: a photograph, apparently. Motive: unknown. Opportunity . . . Leighton was a nobody, a middle-aged civil servant. He earned enough, but not enough to make him blackmail material. He had confided to Rebus that he barely had £2,000 in his building society account.

'Hardly enough to cover their demand,' he had said, as though he were considering actually paying off the blackmailers, even though he had nothing to hide, nothing to fear. Just to get them off his back? Or because he *did* have something to hide? Most people did, if it came down to it. The guilty secret or two (or more, many more) stored away just below the level of consciousness, the way suitcases were stored under beds. Rebus wondered if he himself were blackmail material. He smiled: was the Pope a Catholic? Was the Chief Constable a Mason? Leighton's words came back to him: *Hardly enough to cover their demand.* What sort of civil servant was Leighton anyway? Rebus sought out the day-time telephone number

Leighton had left along with his home address and phone number. Seven digits, followed by a three-figure extension number. He punched the seven digits on his receiver, waited, and heard a switchboard operator say, 'Good afternoon, Inland Revenue.' Rebus replaced the receiver with a guilty silence.

On Tuesday morning, Leighton phoned the station. Rebus got in first.

'You didn't tell me you were a tax man, Mr Leighton.'

'What?'

'A tax man.'

'What does it matter?'

What did it matter? How many enemies could one tax man make? Rebus swallowed back the question. He could always use a friend in Her Majesty's Inland Revenue, for personal as well as strictly professional use . . .

'I know what you're thinking,' Leighton was saying, though Rebus doubted it. 'And it's true that I work in the Collector's office, sending out the demands. But my name's never on the demands. The Inspector of Taxes might be mentioned by name, but I'm a lowly cog, Inspector.'

'Even so, you must write to people sometimes. There might be somebody out there with a grudge.'

'I've given it some thought, Inspector. It was my *first* thought. But in any case I don't deal with Edinburgh.'

'Oh?'

'I deal with south London.'

Rebus noted that, phoning from his place of work, Leighton was less nervous-sounding. He sounded cool, detached. He sounded like a tax collector. South London: but the letters had local postmarks – another theory sealed under cover and posted into eternity, no return address.

'The reason I'm calling,' Leighton was saying, 'is that I had another letter this morning.'

'With a photo?'

'Yes, there's a photo.'

'And?'

'It's difficult to explain. I could come to the station at lunch-time.'

'Don't bother yourself, Mr Leighton. I'll come to the tax office. All part of the service.'

Rebus was thinking of back-handers, gifts from grateful members of the public, all the pubs where he could be sure of a free drink, chip shops that wouldn't charge for a feed, all the times he'd helped out for a favour, the way those favours accumulated and were paid off . . . Tax forms asked you about tips received. Rebus always left the box blank. Had he always been accurate about amounts of bank interest? More crucially, several months ago he had started renting his flat to three students while he lived rent-free with Dr Patience Aitken. He had no intention of declaring . . . well, maybe he would. It helped to know a friendly tax man, someone who might soon owe him a favour.

'That's very good of you, Inspector,' Leighton was saying.

'Not at all, sir.'

'Only it all seems to have been a mistake anyway.'

'A mistake?'

'You'll see when I show you the photograph.'

Rebus saw.

He saw a man and a woman. In the foreground was a coffee-table, spread with bottles and glasses and cans, an ash-tray full to overflowing. Behind this, a sofa, and on the sofa a man and a woman. Lying along the sofa, hugging one another. The photographer had caught them like this, their faces just begin-ning to turn towards the camera, grinning and flushed with that familiar mix of alcohol and passion. Rebus had been to these sorts of party, parties where the alcohol was necessary before there could be any passion. Behind the couple, two men stood in animated conversation. It was a good clear photo, the work of a 35mm camera with either a decent flash-gun or else no necessity for one.

'And here's the letter,' said Leighton. They were seated on

an uncomfortable, spongy sofa in the tax office's reception area. Rebus had been hoping for a sniff behind the scenes, but Leighton worked in an open-plan office with less privacy even than the reception area. Few members of the public ever visited the building, and the receptionist was at the other end of the hallway. Staff wandered through on their way to the coffee-machine or the snack-dispenser, the toilets or the post-room, but otherwise this was as quiet as it got.

'A bit longer than the others,' Leighton said, handing the letter over.

> Mr Leighton,
> Here is the photo. We have plenty more, plus
> negatives. Cheap at £2,000 the lot, and your
> wife will never know. The money should be in
> fives and tens, nothing bigger. Put it in a
> William Low's carrier-bag and go to Greyfriars
> Kirkyard on Friday at 3p.m. Leave the bag
> behind Greyfriars Bobby's gravestone. Walk
> away. Photos and negatives will be sent to
> you.

'Not exactly the quietest spot for a handover,' Rebus mused. Although the actual statue of Greyfriars Bobby, sited just outside the kirkyard, was more popular with tourists, the gravestone was a popular enough stop-off. The idea of leaving a bagful of money there surreptitiously was almost laughable. But at least now the extortion was serious. A time and place had been mentioned as well as a sum, a sum to be left in a Willie Low's bag. Rebus more than ever doubted the blackmailer's professionalism.

'You see what I mean?' Leighton said. 'I can only think that if it isn't a joke, then it's a case of mistaken identity.'

True enough, Leighton wasn't any of the three men in the photo, not by any stretch of the will or imagination. Rebus concentrated on the woman. She was small, heavy, somehow managing to fit into a dress two sizes too small for her. It was black and short, rumpled most of the way to her bum, with plenty of cleavage at the other end. She also wore black tights and black patent-leather shoes. But somehow Rebus didn't think he was looking at a funeral.

'I don't suppose,' he said, 'this is your wife?'

Leighton actually laughed, the sound of paper shredding.

'Thought not,' Rebus said quietly. He turned his attention to the man on the sofa, the man whose arms were trapped beneath the weight of the smirking woman. There was something about that face, that hairstyle. Then it hit Rebus, and things started to make a little more sense.

'I didn't recognise him at first,' he said, thinking out loud.

'You mean you know him?'

Rebus nodded slowly. 'Only I've never seen him smile before, that's what threw me.' He studied the photo again, then stabbed it with a finger. The tip of his finger was resting on the face of one of the other men, the two behind the sofa. 'And I know him,' he said. 'I can place him now.' Leighton looked impressed. Rebus moved his finger on to the recumbent woman. 'What's more, I know her too. I know her quite well.'

Leighton didn't look impressed now, he looked startled, perhaps even disbelieving.

'Three out of four,' Rebus said. 'Not a bad score, eh?' Leighton didn't answer, so Rebus smiled reassuringly. 'Don't you worry, sir. I'll take care of this. You won't be bothered any more.'

'Well . . . thank you, Inspector.'

Rebus got to his feet. 'All part of the service, Mr Leighton. Who knows, maybe *you'll* be able to help *me* one of these days . . .'

Rebus sat at his desk, reading the file. Then, when he was satisfied, he tapped into the computer and checked some details regarding a man who was doing a decent stretch in Peterhead jail. When he'd finished, there was a broad grin on his face, an event unusual enough in itself to send DC Siobhan Clarke sauntering over in Rebus's direction, trying not to get too close (fear of being hooked), but close enough to register interest.

Before she knew it, Rebus was casting her in anyway.

'Get your coat,' he said.

She angled her head back towards her desk. 'But I'm in the middle of—'

'You're in the middle of *my* catchment, Constable. Now fetch your coat.'

Never be nosy, and always keep your head down: somehow Siobhan Clarke hadn't yet learned those two golden rules of the easy life. Not that anything was easy when John Rebus was in the office. Which was precisely why she liked working near him.

'Where are we going?' she said.

Rebus told her on the way. He also handed the file to her so she could read through it.

'Not guilty,' she said at last.

'And I'm Robbie Coltrane,' said Rebus. They were both talking about a case from a few months before. A veteran hard man had been charged with the attempted armed hold-up of a security van. There had been evidence as to his guilt – just about enough evidence – and his alibi had been shaky. He'd told police of having spent the day in question in a bar near his mother's home in Muirhouse, probably the city's most notorious housing scheme. Plenty of witnesses came forward to agree that he had been there all day. These witnesses boasted names like Tam the Bam, Big Shug, the Screwdriver, and Wild Eck. The look of them in the witness-box, police reasoned, would be enough to convince the jury of the defendant's guilt. But there had been one other witness . . .

'Miss June Redwood,' quoted DC Clarke, rereading the casenotes.

'Yes,' said Rebus, 'Miss June Redwood.'

An innocent, dressed in a solemn two-piece as she gave her evidence at the trial. She was a social worker, caring for the most desperate in Edinburgh's most desperate area. Needing to make a phone call, and sensing she'd have no luck with Muirhouse's few public kiosks, she had walked into the Castle Arms, probably the first female the regulars had seen in the saloon bar since the landlord's wife had walked out on him fifteen years before. She'd asked to use the phone, and a man had wandered over to her from a table and, with a wink, had asked if she'd like a drink. She'd refused. She could see he'd had a few – more than a few. His table had the look of a lengthy session about it – empty pint glasses placed one inside another to form a leaning tower, ash-tray brimming with butts and empty packets, the newspaper's racing page heavily marked in biro.

Miss Redwood had given a quietly detailed account, at odds with the loud, confident lies of the other defence witnesses. And she was sure that she'd walked into the bar at 3 p.m., five minutes before the attack on the security van took place. The prosecution counsel had tried his best, gaining from the social worker the acknowledgment that she knew the accused's mother through her work, though the old woman was not actually her client. The prosecutor had stared out at the fifteen jury members, attempting without success to plant doubt in their minds. June Redwood was a rock-solid witness. Solid enough to turn a golden prosecution case into a verdict of 'not guilty'. The accused had walked free. Close, as the fairground saying went, but definitely no goldfish.

Rebus had been in court for the verdict, and had left with a shrug and a low growl. A security guard lay in hospital suffering from shotgun wounds. Now the case would have to be looked at again, if not by Rebus then by some other poor bugger who would go through the same old steps, knowing damned fine who the main suspect was, and knowing that he was walking the streets and drinking in pubs and chuckling at his luck.

Except that it wasn't luck: it was planning, as Rebus now knew.

DC Clarke finished her second reading of the file. 'I suppose you checked on Redwood at the time?'

'Of course we did. Not married, no boyfriends. No proof – not even the faintest rumour – that she knew Keith.'

Clarke looked at the photo. 'And this is her?'

'It's her, and it's him – Keith Leyton.'

'And it was sent to . . . ?'

'It was addressed to a Mr K. Leighton. They didn't get the spelling right. I checked in the phone book. Keith Leyton's ex-directory. Either that or he doesn't have a phone. But our little tax collector is in there under K. Leighton.'

'And they sent the letters to him by mistake?'

'They must know Keith Leyton hangs out in Muirhouse. His mum lives in Muirhouse Crescent.'

'Where does Kenneth Leighton live?'

Rebus grinned at the windscreen. 'Muir*wood* Crescent – only it's not in Muirhouse, it's in Currie.'

Siobhan Clarke smiled too. 'I don't believe it,' she said.

Rebus shrugged. 'It happens. They looked in the phone book, thought the address looked right, and started sending the letters.'

'So they've been trying to blackmail a criminal . . .'

'And instead they've found a tax man.' Now Rebus laughed outright. 'They must be mad, naïve, or built like a hydro-electric station. If they'd *really* tried this bampot caper on with Leyton, he'd have dug a fresh grave or two in Greyfriars for them. I'll give them one thing, though.'

'What's that?'

'They know about Keith's wife.'

'His wife?'

Rebus nodded. 'She lives near the mum. Big woman. Jealous. That's why Keith would keep any girlfriend secret – that's why he'd *want* to keep her a secret. The blackmailers must have thought that gave them a chance that he'd cough up.'

Rebus stopped the car. He had parked outside a block of flats in Oxgangs. The block was one of three, each one shaped like a capital H lying on its face. Caerketton Court: Rebus had once had a fling with a school-dinner lady who lived on the second floor . . .

'I checked with June Redwood's office,' he said. 'She's off sick.' He craned his neck out of the window. 'Tenth floor apparently, let's hope the lift's working.' He turned to Siobhan. 'Otherwise we'll have to resort to the telephone.'

The lift was working, though barely. Rebus and Siobhan ignored the wrapped paper parcel in one corner. Neither liked to think what it might contain. Still, Rebus was impressed that he could hold his breath for as long as the lift took to crackle its way up ten flights. The tenth floor seemed all draughts and high-pitched winds. The building had a perceptible sway, not quite like being at sea. Rebus pushed the bell of June Redwood's flat and waited. He pushed again. Siobhan was standing with her arms folded around her, shuffling her feet.

'I'd hate to see you on a football terrace in January,' said Rebus.

'Some chance.'

There was a sound from inside the door, then the door itself was opened by a woman with unwashed hair, a tissue to her nose, and wrapped in a thick dressing-gown.

'Hello there, Miss Redwood,' said Rebus brightly. 'Remember me?' Then he held up the photograph. 'Doubtless you remember him too. Can we come in?'

They went in. As they sat in the untidy living-room, it crossed Siobhan Clarke's mind that they had no way of proving *when* the photo was taken. And without that, they had nothing. Say the party had taken place after the trial – it could well be that Leyton and June Redwood had met then. In fact, it made sense. After his release, Leyton probably *would* want to throw a party, and he would certainly want to invite the woman who had been his saviour. She hoped Inspector Rebus had thought of this. She hoped he wasn't going to go too far . . . as usual.

'I don't understand,' said June Redwood, wiping her nose again.

'Come on, June,' said Rebus. 'Here's the proof. You and Keith together in a clinch. The man you claimed at his trial was a complete stranger. Do you often get this comfortable with strangers?'

This earned a thin smile from June Redwood.

'If so,' Rebus continued, 'you must invite me to one of your parties.'

Siobhan Clarke swallowed hard. Yes, the Inspector was going to go too far. Had she ever doubted it?

'You'd be lucky,' said the social worker.

'It's been known,' said Rebus. He relaxed into his chair.

'Doesn't take a lot of working out, does it?' he went on. 'You must have met Keith through his mum. You became . . . friends, let's call it. I don't know what his wife will call it.' Blood started to tinge June Redwood's neck. 'You look better already,' said Rebus. 'At least I've put a bit of colour in your cheeks. You met Keith, started going out with him. It had to be kept secret though. The only thing Keith Leyton fears is *Mrs* Keith Leyton.'

'Her name's Joyce,' said Redwood.

Rebus nodded. 'So it is.'

'I could know that from the trial,' she snapped. 'I wouldn't have to know him to know that.'

Rebus nodded again. 'Except that you were a witness, June. You weren't in court when Joyce Leyton was mentioned.'

Her face now looked as though she'd been lying out too long in the non-existent sun. But she had a trump card left. 'That photo could have been taken any time.'

Siobhan held her breath: yes, this was the crunch. Rebus seemed to realise it too. 'You're right there,' he said. 'Any time at all . . . up to a month before Keith's trial.'

The room was quiet for a moment. The wind found a gap somewhere and rustled a spider-plant near the window, whistling as though through well-spaced teeth.

'What?' said June Redwood. Rebus held the photograph up again.

'The man behind you, the one with long hair and the tattoo. Ugly looking loon. He's called Mick McKelvin. It must have been some party, June, when bruisers like Keith and Mick were invited. They're not exactly your cocktail crowd. They think a canapé's something you throw over a stolen car to keep it hidden.' Rebus smiled at his own joke. Well, someone had to.

'What are you getting at?'

'Mick went inside four weeks before Keith's trial. He's serving three years in Peterhead. Persistent B and E. So you see, there's no way this party could have taken place *after* Keith's trial. Not unless Peterhead's security has got a bit lax. No, it had to be before, meaning you *had* to know him before the trial. Know what that means?' Rebus sat forward. June

Redwood wasn't wiping her nose with the tissue now; she was hiding behind it, and looking frightened. 'It means you stood in the witness-box and you lied, just like Keith told you to. Serious trouble, June. You might end up with your own social worker, or even a prison visitor.' Rebus's voice had dropped in volume, as though June and he were having an intimate tête-à-tête over a candlelit dinner. 'So I really think you'd better help us, and you can start by talking about the party. Let's start with the photograph, eh?'

'The photo?' June Redwood looked ready to weep.

'The photo,' Rebus echoed. 'Who took it? Did he take any other pics of the two of you? After all, at the moment you're looking at a jail sentence, but if any photos like this one get to Joyce Leyton, you might end up collecting signatures.' Rebus waited for a moment, until he saw that June didn't get it. 'On your plaster casts,' he explained.

'Blackmail?' said Rab Mitchell.

He was sitting in an interview-room, and he was nervous. Rebus stood against one wall, arms folded, examining the scuffed toes of his black Dr Marten shoes. He'd only bought them three weeks ago. They were hardly broken in – the tough leather heel-pieces had rubbed his ankles into raw blisters – and already he'd managed to scuff the toes. He knew how he'd done it too: kicking stones as he'd come out of June Redwood's block of flats. Kicking stones for joy. That would teach him not to be exuberant in future. It wasn't good for your shoes.

'Blackmail?' Mitchell repeated.

'Good echo in here,' Rebus said to Siobhan Clarke, who was standing by the door. Rebus liked having Siobhan in on these interviews. She made people nervous. Hard men, brutal men, they would swear and fume for a moment before remembering that a young woman was present. A lot of the time, she discomfited them, and that gave Rebus an extra edge. But Mitchell, known to his associates as 'Roscoe' (for no known reason), would have been nervous anyway. A man with a proud sixty-a-day habit, he had been stopped from lighting up by a tutting John Rebus.

'No smoking, Roscoe, not in here.'

'What?'

'This is a non-smoker.'

'What the f— what are you blethering about?'

'Just what I say, Roscoe. No smoking.'

Five minutes later, Rebus had taken Roscoe's cigarettes from where they lay on the table, and had used Roscoe's Scottish Bluebell matches to light one, which he inhaled with great delight.

'Non-smoker!' Roscoe Mitchell fairly yelped. 'You said so yourself!' He was bouncing like a kid on the padded seat. Rebus exhaled again.

'Did I? Yes, so I did. Oh well . . .' Rebus took a third and final puff from the cigarette, then stubbed it out underfoot, leaving the longest, most extravagant stub Roscoe had obviously ever seen in his life. He stared at it with open mouth, then closed his mouth tight and turned his eyes to Rebus.

'What is it you want?' he said.

'Blackmail,' said John Rebus.

'Blackmail?'

'Good echo in here.'

'Blackmail? What the hell do you mean?'

'Photos,' said Rebus calmly. 'You took them at a party four months ago.'

'Whose party?'

'Matt Bennett's.'

Roscoe nodded. Rebus had placed the cigarettes back on the table. Roscoe couldn't take his eyes off them. He picked up the box of matches and toyed with it. 'I remember it,' he said. A faint smile. 'Brilliant party.' He managed to stretch the word 'brilliant' out to four distinct syllables. So it really had been a good party.

'You took some snaps?'

'You're right. I'd just got a new camera.'

'I won't ask where from.'

'I've got a receipt.' Roscoe nodded to himself. 'I remember now. The film was no good.'

'How do you mean?'

'I put it in for developing, but none of the pictures came out. Not a one. They reckoned I'd not put the film in the right way, or opened the casing or something. The negatives were all blank. They showed me them.'

'They?'

'At the shop. I got a consolation free film.'

Some consolation, thought Rebus. Some swop, to be more accurate. He placed the photo on the table. Roscoe stared at it, then picked it up the better to examine it.

'How the—?' Remembering there was a woman present, Roscoe swallowed the rest of the question.

'Here,' said Rebus, pushing the pack of cigarettes in his direction. 'You look like you need one of these.'

Rebus sent Siobhan Clarke and DS Brian Holmes to pick up Keith Leyton. He also advised them to take along a back-up. You never could tell with a nutter like Leyton. Plenty of back-up, just to be on the safe side. It wasn't just Leyton after all; there might be Joyce to deal with too.

Meantime, Rebus drove to Tollcross, parked just across the traffic lights, tight in at a bus stop, and, watched by a frowning queue, made a dash for the photographic shop's doorway. It was chucking it down, no question. The queue had squeezed itself so tightly under the metal awning of the bus shelter that vice might have been able to bring them up on a charge of public indecency. Rebus shook water from his hair and pushed open the shop's door.

Inside it was light and warm. He shook himself again and approached the counter. A young man beamed at him.

'Yes, sir?'

'I wonder if you can help,' said Rebus. 'I've got a film needs developing, only I want it done in an hour. Is that possible?'

'No problem, sir. Is it colour?'

'Yes.'

'That's fine then. We do our own colour processing.'

Rebus nodded and reached into his pocket. The man had already begun filling in details on a form. He printed the letters very neatly, Rebus noticed with pleasure.

'That's good,' said Rebus, bringing out the photo. 'In that case, you must have developed this.'

The man went very still and very pale.

'Don't worry, son, I'm not from Keith Leyton. In fact, Keith Leyton doesn't know anything about you, which is just as well for you.'

The young man rested the pen on the form. He couldn't take his eyes off the photograph.

'Better shut up shop now,' said Rebus. 'You're coming down to the station. You can bring the rest of the photos with you. Oh, and I'd wear a cagoule, it's not exactly fair, is it?'

'Not exactly.'

'And take a tip from me, son. Next time you think of black-mailing someone, make sure you get the right person, eh?' Rebus tucked the photo back into his pocket. 'Plus, if you'll take my advice, don't use words like "reprint" in your blackmail notes. Nobody says reprint except people like you.' Rebus wrinkled his nose. 'It just makes it too easy for us, you see.'

'Thanks for the warning,' the man said coolly.

'All part of the service,' said Rebus with a smile. The clue had actually escaped him throughout. Not that he'd be admitting as much to Kenneth Leighton. No, he would tell the story as though he'd been Sherlock Holmes and Philip Marlowe rolled into one. Doubtless Leighton would be impressed. And one day, when Rebus was needing a favour from the tax man, he would know he could put Kenneth Leighton in the frame.

MIKE RIPLEY

'He writes very much like the early Len Deighton . . .
that sense of street wisdom, weird and wonderful
information and very, very funny.'

Michael Dibdin on KALEIDOSCOPE (Radio 4)

CALLING CARDS

THERE WAS fresh blood on the black guy's hand as he took it
away from his nose. This was probably because I'd just hit him
with a fire-extinguisher.

Well, it wasn't my fault. I'd meant to let it off and blind him
with some disgusting ozone-hostile spray, but could I find the
knob you were supposed to strike on a hard surface? Could I
find a hard surface? Give me a break, I was on a tube train
rattling into Baker Street and I was well past the pint of no
return after an early evening lash-up in Swiss Cottage (what
else is there to do there?). All I could see was this tall, thin
black guy hassling this young schoolgirl. I ask him to desist –
well, something like that – and he told me to mind my own
fucking business, although he wasn't quite that polite.

So, believing that it's better to get your retaliation in first
(Rule of Life No. 59), I wandered off to the end of the compart-
ment and made like I was going to throw up in sheer fright. I
thought I did a fair job of trying to pull the window down on
the door you're supposed to open which links the carriages.
(Think about it – if you're going to throw up, where else do
you do it on a tube?) And, as usual, the window wouldn't open.
So I staggered about a bit, not causing anyone else any grief as
this was late evening and the train was almost empty. And
while swaying about, which didn't take much acting the state
I was in, I loosened the little red fire-extinguisher they thought-
fully tie into a corner by the door.

You can tell someone's put some thought into this, because
it always strikes you that it says 'water extinguisher' when you
know that the tube runs on this great big electric line . . .

Whatever. I got the thing free from its little leather strap and staggered backwards, trying to read the instructions.

After two seconds I gave up and strode down the carriage to where the black guy was sitting and just, well, sort of rammed it in his face, end on.

He couldn't believe it for a minute or two, and neither could I, but I was ready to hit him again. Then he took his hand away from his nose and there was blood all over it. Then his eyes crossed – swear to God, they met in the middle – and then he fell sideways on to the floor of the carriage.

The train hissed into Baker Street station and suddenly there seemed to be lights everywhere. I had a full-time job trying to keep my balance and decide what to do with an unused fire-extinguisher.

The doors of the carriage sighed open and I felt the schoolgirl tugging at my sleeve.

'Come on! Let's blow!' she was yelling. 'He'll be coming at you hair on fire and fangs out once he comes round.'

It seemed a logical argument, the sort you couldn't afford to refuse. So I followed her, dropping the extinguisher on the back of the black guy's head, solving two problems in one.

It made an oddly satisfying noise.

Now to get this straight; she did look like a schoolgirl.

OK, so I'd had a few. More than a few. That's why I'd left my trusty wheels, Armstrong (a black London cab, an Austin FX4S, delicensed but still ready to roll at the drop of an unsuspecting punter), back in Hackney. I had been invited up to Swiss Cottage to a party to launch a rap single by a friend of a friend called Beeby. So you heard it here first; but then again, don't hold your breath.

It had been my idea of lunch – long and free, though I think there was food there too. And round about half-past eight someone had decided we should all go home and had pointed us towards the underground station.

Unfortunately, a rather large pub had somehow been dropped from a spacecraft right into our path and an hour later I found myself on autopilot thinking it was time I got myself home.

So I caught the tube and there I was, in a carriage on one of the side seats (not the bits in the middle where your knees independently cause offences under the Sex Discrimination Act with whoever is opposite) with no one else there except this tall, thin black guy and a schoolgirl, on the opposite row of seats.

At first the guy seemed a regular sort of dude: leather jacket a bit like mine, but probably Marks and Spencers', blue Levis and Reeboks and a T-shirt advertising a garage and spray-paint joint in North Carolina. Nothing out of the ordinary there.

But even in my state I had to do a double-take at the girl he was holding down in the next seat. Not, you note, holding on to or even touching up, but holding down. And when the train hit St John's Wood she waited for the doors to start to close – just like she'd seen in the movies – and then made a break for it. And of course, she didn't make the first yard before he'd grabbed her and sat her down again next to him.

At this point, I lost what remained of my marbles. I interfered.

The thing was, she did look like a schoolgirl. Blue blazer, white shirt straining in all the right places, light blue skirt, knee-length white socks and sensible black shoes. She even had a leather school-satchel-type bag on a shoulder strap and – I kid you not – a pearl-grey hat hanging down her back from its chinstrap.

And this black guy was holding her down. So I asked him to let the young lady go. And he told me where to go. So I got a fire-extinguisher and hit him.

Did I hit him because he was black and somehow defiling a white schoolgirl? Bollocks. Did I step in to protect the fair name of young English maidenhood? Well, it would have been a first.

I did it because I was pissed, but it seemed the right thing to do at the time.

We live and learn.

'Move!' she yelled again as she pulled me down the station towards platform five.

Goodness knows what people thought, though I was in little state to care, as this schoolgirl dragged me down the steps to the Circle Line platform and bustled me into a crowded carriage, all the time looking behind her to see if the black guy was there and only relaxing when the doors closed and the tube shuttled off.

She breathed a deep sigh of relief. I could tell. We were close and the carriage was full. She noticed me noticing.

'I wasn't really in trouble back there,' she said, looking up from under at me in that up-from-under way they do.

'Nah, 'course not.'

I grabbed for the strap handle to keep my balance.

'It was just that Elmore wanted to deliver me – well, had to, really – to somewhere I didn't fancy.'

'That a fact?' I said, which doesn't sound like much but which I regarded as an achievement in my condition.

'You wouldn't understand,' she said quietly, biting her bottom lip.

'You could try explaining. I'm a good shoulder to cry on and I had nothing planned for the rest of the evening.'

Now in many circumstances, that line works a treat. On a crowded Circle Line tube when everybody else has gone quiet and is looking at this suave, if not necessarily upright, young chap chatting up what appears to be the flower of English public schoolgirlhood, it goes down like a lead balloon.

She saved my blushes. In a very loud voice above the rattle of the train she said: 'Then you can take me home.' And then, even louder: 'All the way.'

After that, what could I say?

All the way home turned out to be underground as far as Liverpool Street station, then a mad dash up the escalator and an ungainly climb over the ticket barrier to get to the mainline station just in time to grab two seats on a late commuter bone-shaker heading east.

Trixie lived in one of those north-eastern suburbs which, if it had an underground station, would call itself London, but as it didn't preferred to be known as Essex, but wasn't fooling anyone. There was nobody on duty at the station so we got out without a ticket again and she led me across the virtually deserted Pay-and-Display carpark to a gap in the surrounding fence. That led on to a sidestreet and just went to prove that for early morning commuters the shortest distance between two points is a straight line. I wondered when British Rail would catch on.

Her house was one of a row of two-down, three-ups which backed on to the railway line. The front door had been green once, but the paint had flaked badly and under the streetlights looked like mould. The frame of the bay-window on to the street was in a similar state but through a gap in the curtains I could see a TV flickering.

'Who's home?' I asked, not slurring as much as I had been.

'Josie, my sister. I told you,' she said.

She had too, on the train. Told me of fourteen-year-old Josie who was doing really well at school and had only Trixie to look out for her now that their mum had died. There had never actually been a dad, well not about the house and not for as long as Trixie could remember. And yes, Trixie was her real name, though God knows why, and she was thinking of changing it to something downmarket like Kylie.

She opened the front door and stepped into the hallway, calling out: 'It's me.'

I stepped around a girl's bicycle propped against the wall. It had a wicker carrying-basket on the front in which were a pile of books and one of those orange fluorescent cycling-poncho things which are supposed to tell motorists you are coming.

The door to the front room opened and Josie appeared. She was taller than her sister and she wore a white blouse with slight shoulder pads, a thin double bow tie, knee-length skirt, black stockings and sensible black patent shoes with half-inch heels. She had a mane of auburn hair held back from a clean, well-scrubbed face by a pair of huge round glasses balanced on her head. She held a pencil in one hand and a paperback in the other. I read the title: *The Vision of Elena Silves* by Nicholas Shakespeare. I was impressed.

'You're early,' she said to Trixie, ignoring me.

'This is Roy,' said Trixie.

Josie frowned. 'You know our deal. I'm the only one in this house who does homework.'

'It's not like that, honey. Roy's a friend, that's all. He helped me out tonight, saw me home.'

Josie gave me the once-over. It didn't take long.

'Well, at least you'll be able to press my uniform before school tomorrow,' she said to Trixie.

'Of course, honey, now you get back to your studying and I'll make Roy a cup of tea in the kitchen.'

In the kitchen, she said: 'Don't mind Josie, she doesn't really approve. Put the kettle on while I go and slip into something less comfortable.'

While she was gone, I plugged in the kettle and found tea-bags and sugar. Then I ran some water into the kitchen sink and doused my face, then ran the cold tap, found a mug and drank a couple of pints as a hedge against the dehydration I knew the morning's hangover would bring.

Trixie returned wearing jeans and a sweatshirt, no shoes. She busied herself taking an ironing-board out of a cupboard and setting it up, then plugging in an iron and turning the steam-control up. She began to iron the creases out of Josie's school skirt.

'It was good of you to see me home,' she said conver-sationally.

'Yeah, it was, wasn't it? Why did I do it?'

'And the way you sorted out Elmore . . . I hope he's all right, mind. I've known a lot worse than Elmore.'

Thinking of what I'd done to Elmore made my hands shake.

'You haven't got a cigarette on you?' I asked.

'Sure.' She picked up the school satchel she'd been carrying and slid it across the kitchen table.

I undid the buckles and tipped out the contents: two twelve-inch wooden rulers, five packets of condoms of assorted shapes, flavours and sizes, two packets of travel-size Kleenex, cigarettes, book matches and about a hundred rectangular cards.

I fumbled a cigarette and flipped them.

They were all roughly the same size, about four inches by two, but printed on different coloured card, pink, blue, red, white, yellow and red again. A lot of red in fact. The one thing they had in common was a very large telephone number. Each had a different message and some were accompanied by amateur but enthusiastic line drawings. The messages ranged from STRIKING BLONDE to BLACK LOOKS FROM A STRICT MISTRESS; from BUSY DAY? TREAT YOURSELF to TEENAGER NEEDS FIRM HAND. They all carried the legend 'Open 10 a.m. till late' and 'We Deliver'.

I made a rough guess that we were not talking English lessons for foreign students or New Age religious retreats here.

All the cards had a woman's name on them: Charlotte, Carla, Cherry and so on. I split the pile and did a spray shuffle, then dealt them on to the table like Tarot cards.

'No Trixie,' I said.

'Are you kidding? Who'd believe Trixie? I'm Charlotte and Carla, among others.'

I ran my eye down the cards. Charlotte apparently demanded instant obedience and Carla was an unruly schoolgirl. So much for biographies.

'Working names?' She nodded. 'And tonight was Carla, the one who needs a firm hand?'

'Yeah, but not Mr Butler's.'

'Mr Butler?' I asked, pouring the tea.

'That's where Elmore was taking me. But he didn't tell me it was that fat old git Butler – if that's his name – until we were on the tube. I'd swore I wouldn't do him again, not after the last time. He is *molto disgusto*. Really into gross stuff. He waits till everyone's gone home, then he wants it in the boss's office. I know he's not Mr Butler, but that's what it says on the door.'

'Hold on a minute, what's all this about offices – and where does Elmore come in?'

'It's on the card,' she said taking a cigarette from the packet.

'I've seen hundreds of these things stuck in phone boxes. You ring the number and get told to come round to a block of council flats in Islington,' I said. Then hurriedly added: 'So I'm told.'

'Ah, well, read the difference, sunbeam. "We Deliver" it says.'

The penny dropped. Then the other ninety-nine to make the full pound.

'Elmore delivers you – to the door?'

Trixie blew out smoke.

'To the *doorway* sometimes, but mostly offices, storerooms, hotel rooms. Sometimes carparks, sometimes cinemas. Once even to a box at Covent Garden.'

'You mean one of the cardboard boxes round the back of the flea-market? Which mean sod was that?'

She caught my eye and laughed.

'No, chucklehead, a box at the opera. You wouldn't believe what was playing either. It was a Czech opera called *King Roger*, would you credit it? I thought that was a male stripper.'

'This wasn't one of Mr Butler's treats, was it?'

'Oh no, he's too mean for that. He likes humiliating women, that's his trouble. And I told Elmore never again, but he was just doing what Mrs Glass told him to do.'

'Mrs Glass?'

'Oh, never mind about that.' She turned off the iron and held up Josie's school skirt. 'That's better.'

She folded the board away and joined me at the table, indicating the cards I had laid out.

'Anything there you fancy?' she tried softly.

'Would you be offended if I said no?'

'Too right – I need the money. Josie's expecting to take thirty quid to school tomorrow to pay for music lessons, and I'm skint.'

'Elmore handles the money, right?'

She nodded and ground out her cigarette.

'Are you sure you wouldn't . . .'

I held up a hand, stood up and emptied the contents of my pockets on to the table. As I had been at a freebie all day, I hadn't thought to pack credit cards or anything more than a spot of drinking money. I had £2.49 left, which wouldn't even cover the train fare back to town.

'I was thinking of asking you if you could see your way . . .' I started.

She slapped a hand to her forehead.

'Just my luck,' she muttered under her breath. Then she quietly banged her forehead on the table twice.

'Hey, don't do that. I'll get us some dosh. What time does Josie go to school?'

She looked up. There was a red bruise on her forehead.

'Eight-thirty.'

'No problem. Do you have any black plastic dustbin liners?'

'Yes,' she answered, dead suspicious.

'And some string?' She nodded, biting her lower lip now. 'And an alarm clock?'

'Yeah.' Slow and even more suspicious.

'Then we should be all systems go.'

She gave me a long, hard look.

'I've heard some pretty weird things in my time . . . This had better be good.'

I slept on the couch in the front room and promptly fell off it when the alarm went at six. It took me a couple of minutes to remember where I was and what I was supposed to be doing, and another twenty or so to visit the bathroom as quietly as possible and get it together enough to make some instant coffee.

Then I pulled on my jacket and zipped it up, stuffing the pockets with the dustbin liners and string Trixie had supplied. Over my jacket I attached the fluorescent orange warning strip which I borrowed from Josie's bicycle, then I slung her empty school satchel around my neck to complete the ensemble.

I was ready to go to work.

In the station carpark, I pulled the dustbin liners over the four pay-and-display machines nearest the entrance and secured the open ends with string around the machine posts. It was still dark and I was pretty sure no one from the station saw me.

The first car arrived at quarter to seven and I was ready for it, leaping out of the shadows and holding the satchel out towards the driver's window as he slowed.

'Morning, sir. Sorry about this, the machines are out of action. That'll be two pounds, please.'

It was as easy as that.

After an hour, I got cocky and embellished it slightly. There had been an outbreak of vandalism and the machines had been superglued, or the mainframe was down (whatever that meant) but we were doing our best to repair things.

Then one smartarse in a company Nissan asked for a ticket and when I said I didn't have any, he said 'Tough titties then,' and almost drove over my foot.

He looked just the sort to complain once he got inside the station, though I bet he wouldn't say he parked for free. So I decided to quit while I was ahead. Josie's satchel had so many pound coins in it (no notes as everyone had come expecting a machine) that they didn't rattle any more. It was so heavy, I was leaning to port.

I waited for a gap in the commuter traffic and headed for the hole in the fence. When I got back to Trixie's we counted out £211 on to the kitchen table. I was furious.

At two quid a throw it should have been an even number. One of the early-shift commuters had slipped me an old 5p piece wrapped in two layers of tinfoil.

Somebody should complain to British Rail.

'So what are you going to do now?' I asked, distributing fifty of the coins between two pockets of my jacket and hoping I didn't distress the leather any more.

'Buy some groceries, pay a bill maybe.'

Trixie buttered herself more toast. Josie had taken her music-lesson money, satchel, bicycle and uniform, stuck a slice of toast in her mouth and left without a word to me.

'And then?'

'Oh come on, get real,' said Trixie impatiently. 'Then I ring Mrs Glass and go back to work.'

'When?'

'This afternoon probably.' She glanced at the piles of one-pound coins on the table. 'How long do you think this will last? It'll take a damn sight more to buy me out. This is very useful but it don't make you my white knight or guardian angel.'

I bit my lower lip. I hadn't told her my full name.

She put down her toast but held on to the butter-knife, so I listened.

'I chose to go on the game, so there's no one else to blame. I don't like working for somebody else but I don't have any choice just at the moment, so that's that. OK?'

I picked my words carefully.

'This Mrs Glass, she has something on you?'

'Not her; she just runs the girls from her off-licence in Denmark Street. That's the number on the cards. It's her husband, Mr Glass, who recruits us. And we don't have a choice.'

'Is this Glass guy violent?'

'Not that I've ever seen.' She went back to buttering.

'Then why stick with him? Why not do a runner?'

'He'd find us. He's our Probation Officer.'

I got back to Hackney by noon, in order to collect Armstrong.

The house on Stuart Street was deserted, most of the oddball bunch of civilians who share it with me not yet having given up the day job. Even Springsteen, the cat I share with, was missing, so I opened another can of cat food for him, showered, changed and left before he could reappear. I couldn't face one of his and-where-do-you-think-you-were-last-night? looks.

Before I'd left Trixie's, she'd leaked the basic details of the operation run by Mr and Mrs Glass. Talk about sleazeballs! But then, he who lives by sleaze can get turned over by sleaze and Trixie had given me plenty to go on.

I spent the afternoon sussing out the off-licence on Denmark Street. It wasn't difficult to find, there being only a dozen or so businesses left there now that the developers were moving in. There was just so much time even I could hang around a

Turkish bookshop without raising suspicion, but there were still a handful of music shops left where the leather-jacket brigade could kill a couple of hours pretending to size up fretless guitars and six-string basses.

There was nothing obviously unusual about the off-licence's trade, except that on close inspection there did seem to be a high proportion of young females going in, some of them staying inside for a considerable time. And although they went in singly, they came out in pairs. Not surprisingly, Elmore hadn't turned up for work so the girls were doubling up as their own minders and 'deliverers'. It was time to put in an appearance.

I retrieved Armstrong from around the corner outside St Giles-in-the-Field. As Armstrong is a genuine, albeit delicensed, taxi, there had been no fear of a ticket, even though I had parked illegally as usual. You had to be careful of the privatised wheel clampers, though, as those guys simply didn't care and slapped the old yellow iron boot on anything unattended with wheels.

There wasn't an excess of riches for the shop-lifter, that was for sure. Many of the shelves were almost bare or dotted with mass-market brands of wines – the ones with English names to make ordering easy. Only the large upright cold-cabinet seemed well stocked, mostly with cans of strong lager or 9 per cent alcohol cider which were probably sold singly to the browsers in the next-door music shops.

At the back of the shop was a counter piled with cellophane-wrapped sandwiches, cigarettes and sweets. Behind it, standing guard over a big NCR electronic till was a middle-aged woman who wouldn't have looked out of place serving from a Salvation Army tea-wagon or standing outside Selfridges on a Flag Day for the blind or similar.

'Need any help, love?' she asked. The accent was Geordie, but maybe not Newcastle. Hartlepool, perhaps, or Sunderland.

'Er . . . I'm not sure I'm in the right place,' I said, shuffling from one foot to the other, trying to look like a dork.

To be honest, I suddenly wasn't sure. She looked so – normal.

'Pardon?'

'Well . . . I was told you might have a spot of work going.'

Mrs Glass drew her head back and fiddled with the fake pearls around her neck.

'Work? What sort of work?'

'Err . . . delivering things.' I jerked my head towards the window and Armstrong parked outside. 'I get around quite a bit and a friend said you could always use someone to drop things off.'

'What sort of things?'

'Calling cards.'

She looked me up and down, and then at the till again, just to make sure it was safe.

'Who told you?'

She glanced over my shoulder at Armstrong's comforting black shape. And why not? Policemen, VAT-men, National Insurance inspectors and the Social Security never went anywhere by taxi. Or if they did, they didn't drive it themselves.

'A young lad called Elmore,' I risked.

'When did you see him?'

'Last week sometime.' When he could still speak; before he ate a fire-extinguisher.

She seemed to make a decision. She could have been judging jam at the Mothers' Union.

'It's twenty pounds a throw,' she said, businesslike.

'I thought thirty was the going rate,' I said, knowing that it was at the time.

'You'll be taking the taxi?' I could see her working out the possibilities. Who notices black cabs in London?

'Sure.'

'All right then, thirty. Wait here.'

She fumbled with a key to lock the till and I saw she wore a bunch of them on an expandable chain from the belt of her skirt. She opened a door behind the counter and stepped half in just as a phone began to ring. Holding the door open with one foot, she took the receiver off a wall mount and said 'Hello' quietly. Further in the back room I could see a pair of female feet half out of high heels begin flexing themselves.

Whoever it was must have arrived when I was fetching Armstrong; I hadn't seen anyone else come in. I hoped it wasn't Trixie.

'Why yes, of course Madame Zul is here,' Mrs Glass was saying softly. 'Yes, she is as cruel as she is beautiful. Yes, she is available this afternoon. When and where? Very good, sir. Madame Zul's services begin at one hundred pounds.'

I was straining my ears now and hoping no real customers came in. Not that Mrs Glass seemed in the least bit inhibited. Business was business. 'May I ask where you saw our number? Ah, thank you.'

She concluded her deal and replaced the phone, then, to the girl I couldn't see, she said: 'On yer bike, Ingrid my love. You're Madame Zul this afternoon.'

'Oh, bugger,' said the voice above the feet, the feet kicking the high heels out of my line of sight.

'Sorry, my dear, but Karen's tied up as the naughty schoolgirl.'

Somehow I kept a straight face.

Mrs Glass scribbled something on a sheet of paper and handed it over. A red-nailed hand took it.

'The costume's hanging up and the equipment bag's over there.' Mrs Glass was saying. 'You'd better get a move on.'

Then she turned back to me and she had a Harrods carrier-bag in her hand. She placed it on the counter and turned down the neck so I could see four white boxes, each about three inches by four.

'One of each of these four in every phone box, right?'

I nodded, knowing the score.

'British Telecom only, don't bother with the Mercury phones.'

'Wrong class of customer?' I said before I could stop myself.

She looked at me with a patient disdain normally reserved for slow shop assistants.

'The Mercury boxes are too exposed. They only have hoods, not sides and doors. The cards blow away.'

'Do you use the sticky labels? I've seen those around, you know, the adhesive ones.'

Mrs Glass sighed again, but kept her temper. She was good with idiots.

'If you're caught doing them, you get charged with vandalism 'cos you're sticking something to the box – defacing it. Right? With the cards, all you get done for is littering and they've never prosecuted anyone yet as far as we know.'

'But don't get caught.'

'Right. Now, the cleaners for the Telecom boxes are under contract to clean first thing in the morning every other day. Your patch is Gloucester Place from Marylebone Road down to Marble Arch and don't forget to hit the Cumberland Hotel. There's a bank of phone boxes in there and the place is always full of Greeks. Then work your way over the parallel streets in a square, OK?'

'Baker Street, Harley Street, Portland Place?'

'And don't forget the ones in between. There's a good mixture of foreign students, embassy staff and BBC in that area.'

Again, I thought she might be kidding, but she wasn't. She was obviously proud of her market research.

'We do a random check on you to see that the cards are up. If you're thinking of dumping them, then don't come back. If we don't get a call from one of these boxes within twelve hours, we assume you've dumped them.'

She pulled on her key chain again flipped open the till to remove three ten-pound notes. She pushed them across the counter along with the boxes of calling cards. Then she added a five-pound note.

'Make sure Madame Zul gets to the Churchill Hotel by four o'clock, while you're at it, will you?' Then, over her shoulder, she yelled: 'Ingrid, this nice young man's going to give you a lift!'

Madame Zul, she who was As Cruel As She Was Beautiful, smoked three cigarettes on the way to her tea-time appointment, and as I drew up outside the hotel, she stuffed two pieces of breath-freshening chewing-gum into her mouth, picked up a sports bag which positively clanked, buttoned her trenchcoat around the black plastic outfit she was wearing and stomped off towards the lobby.

I watched her go through the sliding doors, then gunned Armstrong and headed south-east, away from the West End and my card-drop zone.

She had not proved the greatest conversationalist. I had tried a few pleasantries and one obvious chat-up line. I even tried the heavy stuff and asked her whether, as a woman, she felt exploited.

'The punters need us more than we need them,' she answered curtly. 'And I could always work the check-out down the supermarket.'

I was thinking about that, wondering just why I was doing what I was doing, when I arrived at Peter's in Southwark.

Printer Pete's Place is tucked away in a smelly courtyard off Marshalsea Road not a spit away from the old Marshalsea Prison site. Somehow I always suspected Peter – he hated 'Pete' but there had been a typographical cock-up on his business station-ery – took pride in that. He loved dealing in anything shady. Probably that's why he became a printer.

I showed him the boxes of calling cards. I had been prepared to scour the phone boxes of the West End collecting them, but now I had about a thousand in pristine condition, not one thumbed by a sweaty hand.

'Nice enough job,' said Peter, turning one over in his hand. '150 gsm card, centred up, neatly trimmed. Most of the girls working on their own do real hash jobs. It's like trying to see how many different typefaces you can get into six square inches.'

'Can you do what I want?'

'Sure. These babies'll go through the machine easy enough but I'll have to put one of my night-shift on it. This is what we in the trade call a hand job.' He roared at his own joke. 'Hand job, geddit?'

'Not often enough,' I countered.

'Got the numbers?'

I handed over a piece of paper with two 081 London phone numbers and he laid out one of each of the four cards on top of a packing case of printer's ink. The four each had a different catch-line, but the same phone number and the words 'Open 10 till Late' and 'We Deliver'. The messages were: CARLA, TEENAGER, NEEDS FIRM HAND; CHARLOTTE THE STRIKING BLONDE; RELAX IN SAMANTHA'S FIRM HANDS; and, of course, MADAME ZUL, AS CRUEL AS . . . and so on. You know the rest.

'So you want these 081 numbers above the 071 number?' Peter asked.

'If you can overprint easily.' He nodded. 'So how much?'

'A ton,' he said immediately.

'Get outa here,' I responded.

'Seventy-five, then. It's night work. Overtime.'

'Bollocks. Thirty.'

He squinted at me over his wire-frame glasses.

'Any chance of a freebie?' He waved vaguely at the spread of cards.

'Which one?'

He blushed and tapped the MADAME ZUL card with a shaking forefinger. Really, Pete, I had no idea.

'I had that Madame Zul in the back of the cab less than half an hour ago. I can certainly ask for you.'

'Oh then, thirty and you can pick 'em up tomorrow morning, first thing.'

'Thanks Peter, see yer then. But hey – let me tell you, this lady really can be cruel.'

So cruel, she could easily say no.

The best time to catch a Probation Officer is when the pubs and Courts are shut, so I was knocking time spots off a ten-pound phonecard from a booth in King's Cross station by nine the next morning.

He answered his direct line at the third ring.

'Islington Probation Service.'

'Mr Glass? Mr Colin Glass?'

'Yes. Whom am I speaking to?'

'Nobody if you've got this on tape, for your sake.'

There was a pause.

'There's no recording. State your business.'

The accent was northern, unexceptional and not as sing-song as Mrs Glass, your friendly off-licensee.

'I need to talk to you about some of your clients – and before you tell me you don't discuss clients, the ones I'm interested in are Carla, Charlotte, Samantha and Madame Zul, as cruel as . . .'

'Who *is* this?'

'Someone who is going to make you an offer you can't . . .'

'How did you get this number?'

I was getting annoyed with him. He was cutting off all my best lines.

'Get down to York Way in half an hour. Be on the flyover where it goes over the railway. Just walk up and down, I'll find you.'

I hung up and retrieved my phonecard, slotting it back into my wallet along with the white business card from Islington Probation Service which I had lifted from Trixie's handbag.

Very usefully it gave me Mr Glass's direct line at the office, as well as his home phone number.

I noticed an old, half-scraped off adhesive card on the side of the phone. In handwritten lettering it advertised BLACK AND BLUE, THE STRICT TWINS. The number it gave seemed to follow the series of the phone box I was in and for curiosity's sake I checked. It turned out to be four booths away, a distance of maybe twelve feet.

Some people had no imagination.

I cruised up and down York Way, which is just around the corner from King's Cross, until I saw him hop off a bus and begin to look around. He was alone.

I parked Armstrong on the waste-ground which leads to the Waterside pub and Battle Bridge Basin where the longboats attract the groupies in summer (as most are owned by rock musicians) and locked him. I had two pocketfuls of cards, which

I had collected from Peter the printer at 8 a.m.

Being out on the road at that time was almost a first for me. Wearing a suit was another one. I hoped the cards didn't spoil the cut of the double-breasted.

I put on a pair of Ray-bans (fakes, but good fakes) and marched up the road to meet him.

Colin Glass was a worried man. He was about fifty, short and thin and thinning on top. He wore a Man at C & A suit and as it flapped open I could see where a pen had leaked in his inside pocket. I pegged him as a civil servant who had changed to the Probation Service rather than be made redundant from some other department.

'Mr Glass, we need to . . .'

'Just what is going on?' he blustered. 'How dare you ring my office?'

'You'd prefer me to ring you at home?'

I reached into my jacket pocket and he flinched away from me. My hand came out holding a selection of calling cards. I fanned them like a magician.

'Go on, pick a card, any card.'

He picked a blue one: Charlotte, the striking Blonde. One of Trixie's.

'So what the hell is this? What are you trying to say?'

'Ever seen one of those before?' I asked, dead polite.

'Of course not.'

'Check out the phone numbers.'

'Jesus Christ!'

'I doubt it,' I said.

Below us an Inter-City train picked up speed and headed north. Colin Glass looked as if he wished he were on it. Or under it.

'Try another,' I offered, showing him the full wedge of cards from my pocket. Then I reached for my other pocket. 'Or how about teenagers in need of a firm hand, or Madame . . .'

'Who . . . did . . . this?' he spluttered.

'I have no idea, but unless certain things happen, about a thousand of these things will hit the phone boxes this afternoon and there could be a specially targeted drop in certain areas of Islington. Not to mention a few through the post to various people.'

He was ashen now, but still holding the cards at arms length as if they would bite.

'There's . . . can we . . . ?'

'How many girls have you working for you, Colin? And do tell the truth. You know it makes sense.'

'Six in all.'

'All clients of yours?' He nodded. 'All on probation?'

'They are . . . or they were.'

'That's naughty, isn't it, Colin. Abusing your position and all that. What a story for the newspapers, eh?'

'Look, they were on the game anyway. If anything we made it safer for them, made them pool their efforts.' He was trying out arguments he'd rehearsed but hoped never to use. He wouldn't look me in the face.

'And I bet Mrs Glass made them cups of tea and saw to it that they had condoms on tap and probably did a bit of counselling on the side.'

He looked up and there was a faint spark of hope in his dead-fish eyes. I blew it out.

'Tell it to the judge. And the papers. And the Civil Service Commission.'

He bit his lower lip.

'What is it you want?'

'You out of business, that's what. This afternoon. Close up the Denmark Street shop – man, that's so obvious a front I'm surprised you haven't been raided by the drugs squad. Rip the phone out and pay off all the girls. Give them a grand each, cash. Call it their redundancy money.'

'Six thousand? I can't . . .'

'You will. Where's all the profit gone, eh?'

'You don't understand . . . the pension they give is pathetic.'

'Stay lucky and you might get one. If you don't come across by four o'clock this afternoon, these things go out.' I waved some more cards at him. 'By breakfast tomorrow you'll be giving press conferences – and so will your bosses. Mind you, look on the bright side. Your wife could pick up a bit of business overnight once this number here . . .'

'All right, all right, I'll do it.'

'Remember, a thousand to each girl. Got anyone else working for you?'

'No.'

I dropped a couple of the cards on the pavement and he scuttered after them before they blew into the gutter, moaning 'No, please . . .'

'How about a dude called Elmore?'

'Only him. He sub-contracts jobs when he has to.'

'Then a grand for him too and tell him to retire. If any of them ask, just say it was a present from a Guardian Angel, got that?'

He stood up again, the knees of his trousers filthy from where he'd scrabbled on the pavement.

'Why are you doing this to me?' he asked nervously. 'What's in it for you?'

I looked up and down York Way. There was no one else in sight and traffic was light. I slipped my left hand into my jacket pocket.

'There's nothing in it for me,' I grinned. 'And I'm doing it because I don't like your attitude. You're supposed to be one of the good guys.'

It was the only answer I could think of and I didn't want to debate it, so I threw a fistful of his calling cards into the air and left him on his knees again, frantically trying to pick up every last one.

I told the story to my old and distinguished friend Bunny in a pub in Hackney about two months later.

Bunny is very interested in all matters female and feminist and for all the wrong reasons. He regards it the same way as opposing generals regard intelligence on troop movements.

'But what did you get out of it, Angel? A quick bonk?'

'Just a good feeling,' I said, not really knowing myself.

'So you did get to . . .'

'Please, curb that one-track mind of yours.'

'I can't help it if I'm over-healthy.'

I spluttered into my beer.

'What's wrong with that, then?'

'Nothing,' I choked.

We had got on to this subject because Bunny had found a red calling card stuck in the door frame by the pub's public phone. I hadn't read it properly until now.

'Well, I think it shows great initiative,' he was saying. 'A working girl's got to work, so why not employ the latest technology?'

He was referring to the card which listed an 0860 number – a mobile phone.

I read the legend: CARLA, TEENAGER, NEEDS A FIRM HAND.

I suddenly knew how Trixie had spent her redundancy money.

DAVID WILLIAMS

'David Williams weaves a deceitful tale with the
best of them.'

SUNDAY TIMES

TAKE TWO
HUSBANDS

'THIS PAPER'S got nothing but sex in it,' plain Maud Guttins
protested, noisily turning the pages.

'Court reports, is it, dear?' her husband Lancelot Guttins commented tentatively. He vaguely wished she might be right, but
knew she wasn't. He put more marmalade on his breakfast toast.
It was too much to hope that the *Tidcombe Times* had gone over
entirely to pornography.

'Too many of the court reports simply cater for the prurient,'
Maud went on. 'It's not even normal sex either. Not most of it.'

You had to admire the way she could complain, and read, and
slurp up Weetabix all more or less at the same time. 'Can I have
some more coffee, dear?' he asked, wondering exactly what, in
view of her limited experience, Maud would recognise as abnor-
mal sex.

She took his cup and poured the coffee.

*It was at that moment that he saw the kitchen door fly open. Then he
watched, powerless, as a group of shouting leather-jacketed junkies
burst in, overturned the table, and forced the screaming Maud to the
floor, ripping off her clothes, and ravishing her in front of him.*

This sequence was Mr Guttins' favourite Maud imagining.
The intruders were sometimes American Indians in full war
paint, or jackbooted Nazi SS, or fiends from outer space. What
followed after their entry was always more or less the same.

'Of course, sex before marriage is the absolute norm these
days,' Maud went on, unaware of the awful fate that had just
befallen her, and handing back the cup. 'The absolute norm.'

Mr Guttins sighed quietly. It was sex *after* marriage that had been upsetting Maud for the last twenty-five of her forty-eight years. Pretty well since she had given birth to Kevin – after doing her bit, as her mother had put it so cogently at the time. Kevin was married himself now. An engineer, he had emigrated to Australia, which was just as well because his wife hadn't got on with Maud.

'Isn't it time you were going, Lancelot?'

'Yes, dear.'

Dark, with plenty of hair still, a small moustache and kind eyes, Mr Guttins was a wiry man, and small, a touch smaller even than his wife, but more energetic. There was a spring in his step as he got outside into the June sunshine. He was dressed conservatively in the style he thought befitted a retail pharmacist. He stopped to pluck a yellow rosebud from one of the floribunda bushes along the drive, doing so expertly with the penknife from his pocket. Gardening was his nominal hobby. But for real escape he relied on sexual fantasy.

He looked back at the house as he closed the gate behind him. It was solid, detached, double-gabled, and red-brick, standing in its own bit of garden like its identical neighbours in this solid red-brick seaside town in the south of England. You couldn't see the ocean from here, in inappositely named Nelson Avenue, but you could smell it when the wind was right.

Mr Guttins fixed the rose in the lapel of his clerical grey jacket, adjusted the black-banded straw hat on his head, and made off down the avenue with short, quick steps. It was an eleven and a half-minute steady walk to Pembroke's, the chemist's shop he managed on the eastern side of the town, near the sea-front. He was not obliged to walk. There was a frequent bus service from the corner which he sometimes used in the winter, and very occasionally Maud drove him to work in their year-old Rover 200. Mostly though he chose to walk. He said it was healthier. In fact it was because he could thus more easily attend to the needs of the young women along the route who daily begged him to undress them – as well as to do other things to them afterwards.

Of course, the begging was in the same category of imagining as the leather-jacketed junkies. Mr Guttins was a pathetically frustrated middle-aged husband with a frigid wife. The exciting sex life he led was entirely in his mind.

Fourteen minutes after leaving the house he was inserting the key in the front door of the shop. The walk had taken longer than need be on account of an extra two-minute interlude, nominally to tighten both his shoelaces alongside the municipal tennis courts.

Two nubile and already minimally clothed girls had been out for an early game at the courts. He had indulged their brazen pleadings to strip them both, meeting their entreaties with deft, practised hand movements. He had enjoyed revealing the stark and lovely flesh, but left the creatures begging for the more intimate satisfactions which they had wanted next.

'Excuse me? Do say you're opening the shop now?'

The stunning young woman who had spoken was struggling to get out of the low Mercedes Coupé parked at the kerb across the narrow pavement in front of Pembroke's. Mr Guttins turned in her direction at the very moment when her long legs – clad in sheer black panty-hose under the shortest of red skirts – had parted, a trifle indelicately, to ease the movement of the rest of her remarkable body.

It was a moment before he could utter. His thoughts had still been savouring his adventure with the abandoned tennis players. He pointed to the notice on the door and without taking his eyes off this fresh, real personification of loveliness, not to mention lust. 'Officially, we're not open till nine,' he said at last, already in his mind wresting the last flimsy garment from her willing body. Then he smiled nervously and doffed his hat, feeling his cheeks redden in response to the exciting contraction in his loins as she stood before him, to his perception, naked and unashamed.

'It's a prescription. For' – she paused momentarily, the big brown eyes considering Mr Guttins more carefully than before – 'for my husband. For his heart. I tried to get it filled last night. The chemist I went to didn't stock it.' Standing beside him, she shook the mass of bouffant blonde hair before opening her white leather handbag. She pouted a little as she searched for something in the bag, her tongue running around her lips and making them shine. 'Here it is,' she said, looking up. Her white V-necked collarless blouse was bursting at the front, revealing under the open top two buttons not only a generous amount of cleavage but also a breathtaking treat of firm, genuinely unencumbered bosom.

Mr Guttins started undressing her all over again.

'Urgent, is it?' he asked, swallowing and taking the prescription from the long, tapering fingers that touched his with a quite electric effect. The perfume she was wearing was for him more provocative than any advertisement could have claimed for it: it also smelled more expensive than anything stocked at Pembroke's.

'It's terribly urgent.' She moved even closer to him, as if they were sheltering from a sudden shower under the narrow lintel above the shop door.

'I see it's a repeat private prescription.' He pretended to reread the words so that his eyes could continue to feast on the genuinely unencumbered bosom.

'From my husband's Harley Street doctor. For quite a small amount of—'

'Digoxin syrup. Yes. It's not a proprietary. I mean I'll have to make it up for you.' He went on seeming to study the writing. 'It's just for a week's supply.'

She nodded. 'That's why I'm always having to get a fresh lot.'

'Well, it's quite strong stuff. You don't want too much of it lying about.' He glanced at his watch. It was 8.41. 'Come inside, won't you? I think we can manage it all right.'

He ushered her through into the shop ahead of him – *thrusting himself into her in response to her insistent cries for more.*

'I'll have to close the door again, I'm afraid. My assistant doesn't get here till nine. There's a chair if you want. I'll just . . . yes.' He went behind the counter, then unlocked the glass door into the dispensary beyond.

'I'm intruding on your quiet time, I expect?'

'No, no, not at all. That is—' He looked up to find her standing in the dispensary doorway. 'Oh, I'm afraid—'

'I mustn't come any further? Of course not. It's just that I adore the atmosphere of chemist shops. Especially a small one like this. With such a dear little old-fashioned dispensary.'

'We're old-fashioned all right.' He took off his suit jacket, *then, nonchalantly, everything else he had on.* He hung up the jacket and, turning full frontal to face her, languidly put on his white-cotton working-jacket – treating it like the sexy silk dressing-gown he imagined it had become. *He heard her catch her breath*: well, that was understandable.

Indeed, Mr Guttins was not in the least surprised at the increasingly approving gaze that in reality the woman was keeping on him: it came so close to the way she looked at him in his fantasy.

'Old Mr Pembroke, the owner, won't change anything if he can help it. Or modernise. He has three shops like this one,' the pharmacist continued, perfectly able to carry on normal conversations and mundane activities while indulging in an imaginary orgy.

'Quite a little chain.'

'Along the coast, yes. This is the only one in Tidcombe.' He did up the lower button of the white jacket while imagining he was loosely knotting the dressing-gown sash.

'A gold-mine, is it?'

His hands gave an uncertain gesture as he looked along a line of drawers above the dispensing table. 'That's not my province, I'm afraid. I make this shop pay. I've been here over fifteen years. It suits me,' he ended lamely.

'Good for you. You're married I see.'

He glanced down at the wedding ring she had noticed. 'Yes. For a little longer than fifteen years.' He gave a chuckle, not knowing quite why, then his expression changed. 'Oh, dear, I'm afraid I don't have enough Digoxin to fill the prescription.'

'Oh sh— too bad,' she responded, the tapered fingers pulling at the long gold chain that was glinting enticingly in her cleavage – unaware that Mr Guttins had whipped her bare buttocks with it while they'd still been out on the pavement.

'Look, why not take what I can make up? That's about a day's dosage. Then come back this afternoon for the rest?' he suggested. 'I can easily get a fresh supply during the day. I mean if that's convenient.'

She frowned. 'It means driving down again from Hightops. And you know what the traffic's like in the afternoon. I think I'd better—'

'Hightops? That's on my route home. Or nearly,' he put in quickly, and inaccurately. Hightops was the exclusive section of town, a good deal out of his way, and a steep climb – except Mr Guttins would have scaled Everest barefoot for the chance of seeing this vision again. 'I could bring the rest of the prescription with me. That's if you wouldn't mind paying for all of it now?' He still remembered to ensure observance of the shop rules.

'Could you? You are sweet. Of course I'll pay now. Tell me how much.' She opened her bag again. 'And I'll give you directions to the house. Our name's Hallier, by the way. Well, you can see that from the prescription. I'm Kate Hallier.'

It was a little after 5.45 when Mr Guttins arrived sweating at the house in Hightops. The steep, bending drive was cut deep into the chalk soil – banked, and sheltered by conifers on both sides. The visitor came upon the north, entrance, front of the building quite suddenly, and, despite his determination, it must be admitted gratefully, as he emerged beyond the last line of trees. It was a substantial house, too high up to be overlooked – a 1930s flat-roofed villa, rendered in white, with a marvellous view of the sea to the south.

'You walked? You poor lamb. I thought—'

'I like to walk.' He was carrying his jacket when she opened the door to him. 'I've brought the prescription.'

'Never mind that. Come in for a drink. Unless you have to hurry home. To your wife. I'm sitting by the pool. It's still lovely and hot there.'

Mrs Hallier was wearing a thigh-length diaphanous yellow wrap which she was still tying in a bow at the neck. Underneath Mr Guttins could make out the briefest of matching bikini briefs through the parting in the wrap. It didn't seem that she had the bikini top on, but it was difficult to be sure the way the wrap material was bunched. But because she was so close to being unclothed already, he had no need to make believe he was stripping her.

'Thank you. I'd like that. I'd like that very much. My wife has her bridge always on Tuesdays. And . . . and on Wednesdays,' he added unnecessarily. He had started to sweat again, but now it wasn't from the exertion of the climb.

'And this is Tuesday.' She smiled tolerantly.

'Yes. So there's no hurry. None at all. What a very nice house.'

'We like it. We're renting it this year, with a view to buying. It's *very* private.' She took his arm as she guided him through the square hall, across the drawing room, and through sliding windows onto a wide paved terrace. A kidney-shaped swimming-pool was sheltered and suntrapped below the terrace, down some curved stone steps. 'My husband's supposed to be living in a warm climate. We should have gone to Florida or Italy, but he insists on carrying on with his business. And he doesn't like flying any more. Or being too far from his British doctors. He's older than me. Seventy-six.' Mr Guttins, in thrall to the grip on his arm, calculated that this made her husband older by about fifty years. 'Tidcombe is the compromise,' she added.

'Could I ask what business your husband's in?'

'Antique furniture. The pricey kind. He has a gallery in Bond Street. He's there now. Seeing an American client.'

'Oh, from what you said this morning, I thought—'

'He left at lunch-time. With . . . with the chauffeur. Back Thursday. That's his routine mid-week. We have a flat above the gallery. But I hate London. Especially in summer.'

'He'll need his Digoxin syrup?'

'No, he has enough to last him. With what you gave me this morning,' she said as they went down the steps to the poolside. 'Let me take your jacket. Would you like a swim? The water's heated to a sinful ninety degrees.'

'I . . . I haven't brought a costume.'

She shrugged. 'That really doesn't matter up here. If you want, I expect there's a spare one in the changing-room over there.'

'Next time perhaps.' He was ashamed at his lack of courage.

'If that's a promise. With your physique, I'll bet you're a fabulous swimmer.' She smiled, squeezed his arm muscle, then stood away from him a little to look him up and down, still in her warmly appraising way.

'Hardly that,' he replied with more justification than he intended. 'I used to swim a lot. Tennis was . . . is my sport really.'

'I like tennis too. Pity we don't have a court here. Sit over there then, and I'll get you that drink. Whisky, gin?' She waved her hand at a raffia-bound drinks trolley behind them near the steps.

'Gin and tonic. Thank you.' He sat awkwardly and sideways on one of two long white mattressed lounger-chairs set only inches apart, and half shaded by a huge sun-umbrella. He was feeling overdressed and aware he should at least remove his shoes if he was going to sit properly. He had dealt with the shoes but was still trying to settle himself on the chair when she came back with his drink.

'Topless doesn't embarrass you does it? You being a medical man? The English generally are so prudish about that kind of thing.'

'No, no . . . I mean, not at all,' he answered weakly in a strained voice, while trying to cloak both his embarrassment and his excitement.

She had discarded the wrap and was now standing over him quite naked except for the slim bikini briefs. Her breasts were firm and bronzed like the rest of her. He swallowed and took the glass. This was the most erotic experience of his whole life – and it beat the hell out of his fantasies.

On Mr Guttins' second visit, on the following Tuesday at the same time, Mrs Hallier casually led her guest into a mutual exchange of intimate confidences about their lives. This revealed that they were equally disenchanted with their marriages.

It was not until Mr Guttins' third visit, on Wednesday the day after that, and when there could be no pretence that he was bringing a prescription for her husband, that the intimate exchanges took the form of actions, as well as words. This might have happened earlier, but Mrs Hallier had been determined not to rush things unduly. Now the lounger-chairs were pushed tightly together like a double bed. Mr Guttins had arrived in time for the light lunch she'd prepared by the pool – smoked salmon, then strawberries, with champagne to drink. It was early closing in Tidcombe on Wednesdays. He had told Maud he wouldn't be home for lunch because he was stock-taking: Maud was at her bridge club from four o'clock to seven.

'But I told you, I've always preferred older men,' Kate Hallier protested later as they lay naked, side by side in the sun, still sipping the champagne. Earlier he had been wearing the swimming shorts she had found for him the day before. He assumed they belonged to her husband. They had been a touch too big for him – but easy for her to pull off him later, when they had been playing in the pool. 'Well, slightly older men,' she enlarged. 'Men your age, for instance. It's just that Cedric's too old for . . . well, you know . . . almost everything really.' She ran a hand down his hairless chest, then on to his thigh, her nails scoring the flesh.

Mr Guttins gave a contented moan. 'But he's rich,' he said. Cedric Hallier was certainly decrepit-looking as well as old. Kate had produced a photograph of herself with the old boy taken at the pool. She had been hugging him like a sugar daddy: Mr Guttins had found the picture obscene.

'Being rich isn't everything,' said Kate. 'You're much better off than he is, really. You're the perfect age. You have your health and strength, a good job, nice home, I expect, despite—'

'But I don't have a gorgeous wife like you to have . . . to have sex with.' He still had to force out the franker phrases. He had never before talked to a woman in the way he talked to this one. His fantasies had not involved much conversation. The present experience was as liberating as making love to Kate – or almost.

'That's easily fixed, silly. You could divorce Maud. Marriage doesn't have to be for ever, you know?'

'But I've no one else to go to.'

'Aren't I good enough? I'd marry you. Or live with you.'

'But you hardly know me!'

She put her glass to one side and, leaning over him, kissed him slowly on the lips. 'Except I was crazy about you the moment I saw you. Didn't you notice? I don't go in for casual affairs. Not my style, darling. But you are.' Her finger traced an outline on his forehead, then his cheek. 'This is the first time I've ever been unfaithful to Cedric. I've been tempted, of course. I've told you how awful it's been for me all these years.' There was a catch in her throat so that he thought she might be about to cry, until she went on more firmly. 'I've been waiting for you to come along. For longer than I can tell you. You're perfect, my sweet. We're perfect together.' She kissed him again.

Of course, he wanted to believe her. She had made his imaginings come true: all of them – and better than just true. 'But you wouldn't divorce Cedric for me?' It was less a question than a supplication.

She lay her head back on the cushion. 'You said the Pembroke shops are for sale.' Her tone was thoughtful, and implied that she wasn't changing the subject.

'Mr Pembroke wants to sell, yes. It's common knowledge in the town. But he can't get his price.'

'Wouldn't you like to be the buyer?'

'Yes,' he answered boldly. 'And . . . and I'd know how to run the shops too. I mean much better than they're being run now.' In fact he'd never once thought of himself in the role of proprietor of anything. Simply, she had the effect of spurring him on recklessly to undreamed of goals – to a new kind of fantasy.

Kate sighed. 'What an idyllic life. To own a nice little group of chemist's shops. Traditional ones. And live right here.'

'No chance of that, I'm afraid,' he responded. 'Mr Pembroke wants nearly a million pounds for the three. He won't sell them separately either.'

'Cedric's worth ten times that.'

Mr Guttins gave a despondent murmur. 'But he's not likely to buy them for me is he?' he offered flatly.

'But I will, when Cedric's dead. I promise. I inherit everything.' She rolled her body back toward his. Her hand moved down his chest. 'Pity we can't kind of hurry him along.'

'To his . . . to his death, you mean?' Although he had

hesitated over the word death, for some reason such an appalling proposal didn't seem appalling to him at all, not at that moment. It was like one of his imaginings, where there were no consequences.

'Yes. It'd be doing him a favour. He's getting no pleasure out of life, and he's often in great pain. But they won't operate on his heart. He wouldn't survive. Well, that says it, doesn't it?' She pressed herself even closer to him as her hand moved lower. 'He's just longing for the end, really. The work keeps his mind off things, that's all. Yes, it'd be a kindness. I know just the way to do it too.'

'You mean you'd want me to—'

'No darling, I'd handle it alone. It'd be nothing to do with you. Not the actual ending.'

'But how—?'

She stopped his words by placing her other hand over his mouth. 'Tell you later,' she murmured, kneeling astride him then bending down to run her tongue slowly down his stomach. 'Something more urgent's coming up.'

'You'd need to make up two prescriptions that look the same, with the same dates on the labels. But one would be his normal Digoxin, and the other very high strength Digoxin. Lethal strength. It'll need to be that.' She seemed to savour the word lethal.

They were lying side by side again in the sunshine as she went on. 'I'd put the normal-strength bottle in his bathroom cabinet on the first night. That'd be a Thursday.'

'You have separate bathrooms? And . . . and bedrooms?'

'Er . . . yes. Because of Cedric's snoring. He'd take the dose as usual, so his fingerprints would be on the bottle. That could be important. He takes just the one dose at night. Well, you know that. On the Friday, I'd switch the bottle for the high-strength one. After pouring out enough of what's in it to make the levels the same. So he couldn't notice any difference.' She paused. 'Then when . . . when it's all over, when he's gone, I get rid of the second bottle, and put the first one in its place. That's after I've poured away most of what's in it. It'll just look as if he's taken too much.'

'By mistake or on purpose?' Mr Guttins asked quickly.

'No one could ever know for certain, could they?' She stretched her arms above her head. 'He likes the taste. I always think he's going to take too much anyway.' She turned her head to look at Mr Guttins. 'That'd work wouldn't it?'

He swallowed. He was in awe at the way she had everything so clear in her mind. 'Yes, it should work all right,' he said. 'And it's so simple. Is it too simple, d'you think?'

'Simple schemes are always the best. No complicated trimmings to go wrong.' She had answered with the same authority as before.

'You say he's never been to a doctor in Tidcombe?'

'No. Only in London.'

'In that case, if he died here there'd have to be a post-mortem.'

She pushed herself up on her elbows. 'So they'd find he'd taken too much of his syrup. It's what they'd be expecting. It'd be his fault he'd taken too much.'

'So long as they didn't think you'd given him an overdose.'

'How could I do that? Hold him down and pour it into him? Lace his coffee with it? Nearly a whole bottle? It'd take that much, wouldn't it.'

'In the normal strength, yes.'

'So he'd have known straight away. Anyone would with that quantity. And it has a very distinctive taste. And smell.'

'That's true.' It still bothered him that she could be suspect. But he wanted her plan to work more than anything else in the world. He was already imagining life with her in this house. 'People won't think it odd when we get married later?' he asked, but confident that she'd have the answer to that too.

'Only if we did it straight away. Of course, we'd have to wait a decent interval.'

'But how would we sort of . . . come together, even then? I mean, when would I leave Maud?'

'Oh, that's easy. Once Cedric's gone, I'd have my solicitors buy all the shops from Mr Pembroke. As a straightforward investment. I'd appoint you general manager, so we'd have to meet. Often. At the shops and here. One thing would lead to another. We'd fall in love. You'd leave Maud. She'd divorce you. We'd marry, and live here happily ever after.'

'Yes,' he said eagerly. 'Yes,' willing it all to come true – imagining that it had.

'Yes, of course, Doctor Chalcott, I'll come right away. It's no trouble,' Mr Guttins had said into the telephone ten minutes before this. It had been just after six-thirty on Saturday morning. 'No I understand perfectly, Doctor. Better to get it cleared up straight away. Less distressing for the relatives . . . Yes, I agree. See you shortly then.'

The call had woken him. They usually slept in an extra half-hour on Saturdays because he opened the shop later that day. Maud, in the other bed, had wanted to know why Dr Chalcott was calling. She knew Dr Chalcott. He wasn't the Guttins' doctor, but he practised in the town, in the Hightops district.

Mr Guttins had explained things briefly to his wife. A Mr Cedric Hallier had died suddenly. He had a prescription for the treatment of a heart condition filled at Pembroke's every week. Dr Chalcott had been called in. He was at the dead man's house now and wanted the prescription identified. That had satisfied Maud who had gone back to sleep.

Mr Guttins had dressed quickly and was now in the Rover driving to the house in Hightops. He hadn't been there for ten days – not since his fourth visit which Kate had made even more memorable than the others. That had been two Wednesdays ago, a week after Kate had proposed the plan to have Cedric kill himself. Mr Guttins had thought then that despite his desire for Kate, that once he was away from her, his resolve to see the thing through might crumble. But on his visit a week later he had been keener than ever.

He had accepted that he hardly ran any risk at all. The only danger was still that Kate might be suspected of giving the overdose. But in a wishful thinking way, Mr Guttins had managed to detach himself from the consequences of that happening.

It was on that final visit that he had delivered the extra-strong prescription of Digoxin. He had dated the label for the second Thursday following – and put a smudge of red ink in the label's right-hand corner. That had been to make it easy for Kate to identify. It wouldn't do to mix the two bottles.

No one he knew had ever seen Mr Guttins enter or leave the sheltered driveway of the house at Hightops. Kate had questioned him carefully on that, but he'd been quite sure. The road had very few houses in it, and he'd remembered distinctly it having been empty on his first visit. On subsequent visits he had been feeling far too guilty to enter when anyone was looking. And he had never told Heather, his unglamorous assistant in the shop, about the special deliveries either.

Kate had come in to the shop for the normal Digoxin prescription on Thursday, two days ago. It had been mid-morning and she had handed the form to Heather, who had passed it to Mr Guttins. He had been in the dispensary at the time and had remarked pointedly to Heather that Mrs Hallier had been in before for the same reason. He had even come out of the dispensary to wish Mrs Hallier the time of day after he had prepared the bottle of syrup.

And now, he assured himself, it was all over bar the shouting. He could hardly believe it.

The Rover took the steep drive in its stride, soaring to the top with the same sort of zest that its driver was experiencing. He parked beside Dr Chalcott's big Volvo. It was Dr Chalcott he had told Kate to call when the time came. He was one of the older practitioners in the town, a bluff individual who could be relied on to draw the obvious inferences from the facts presented. And the doctor had made that plain enough to Mr Guttins on the telephone.

'Come in, old chap. Nice to see you. Sorry to get you out of bed.' It was Chalcott who answered the door. 'A word in your ear.' The benign, heavily built doctor drew the pharmacist aside in the hall before continuing in a lowered voice. 'Probably a simple cardiac arrest, but he just could have swallowed too much of that anti-congestive you've been supplying.'

'Signs of that, you said?' the pharmacist commented, in the

professional tone he used in the shop when old ladies asked for advice on the best choice of cough mixture.

'Hm, some signs.' The doctor sniffed. 'Possibly just my suspicious mind. Chap's heart condition finally did for him, I expect. Knew him did you?'

'No. Mrs Hallier picked up the prescription every week.'

'Did she now? Attractive woman. Very distressed she's been. They must have been close. More so than you'd expect, really.' The doctor's eyebrows rose in a questioning way to punctuate what, to Mr Guttins, had seemed slightly curious observations. 'She showed me the prescription. From some Harley Street quack. Limited to a week's supply, presumably because the old boy wasn't to be trusted with more. In case he did himself a mischief? That's the thing that made me wonder. I see you've dated the prescription on the back each time you've dispensed it. Very proper.'

'The last time was on Thursday. So you think he might have taken an overdose?'

The doctor made a noise with his tongue like water dripping on to stone. 'Post-mortem will show it if he did. There'll have to be one, of course. I gather he was wealthy.' He made the dripping noise again. 'Another reason to be sure everything's er . . . on the up and up. So if you could just have a look at that Digoxin, then the body can go straight to the hospital morgue. We're in the kitchen. There's coffee going.' He led the way along the hall.

'It's Mr Guttins, isn't it?' said Kate as they entered the kitchen. She was seated at the table. A dark, handsome man of about her own age was standing behind her. Mr Guttins assumed that this was the chauffeur who, of course, he hadn't met, although there was something vaguely familiar about the face. There was a coffeepot and several cups on the table. Kate and the man were both in dressing-gowns – Kate's being a frilly, glamorous affair in white nylon. She looked as if she had been crying.

To Mr Guttins Kate looked like the most desirable woman on earth – and she was all his, no kidding, no fantasies.

'Good morning, Mrs Hallier,' he responded. 'I'm sorry to hear the sad news.'

'You're very kind.' She touched her eyes with the tissue in her hand. 'He seemed so well last night. Then Jack took him a cup of tea early, as usual, and found him dead.' She looked up at the man behind her. 'It was a terrible shock for us both.'

'We won't keep you much longer, Mrs Hallier,' said the doctor. 'I just want Mr Guttins to have a look at the bottle of Digoxin over here.' He moved across to the working top under the window and picked up the brown glass container. 'Dated the fifteenth,' he said. 'That's two days ago.' He held the bottle up to the light. 'And a quarter of the contents consumed. Or a bit less than that. Which is as it should be.' He handed the bottle to the pharmacist. 'Shows the patient hadn't taken too much by mistake. Certainly not from this bottle. That about right, Mr Guttins?'

Mr Guttins stared at the bottle, opened his mouth, but no words came out. He had been disturbed at how full the bottle was. Now his gaze was riveted on the red ink-smudge on the label. It was the bottle with the high-strength mixture.

'So it was a heart-attack, doctor?' asked the man behind Kate. It dimly registered with the preoccupied Mr Guttins that the accent was more cultured than you would normally expect in a chauffeur. 'Perhaps my father should have been taking more of the medicine, after all. My wife was always impressing on him not to overdo that stuff, weren't you, darling?' He put both his hands on Kate's shoulders.

'Patients like the taste of Digoxin syrup, Mr Hallier,' the doctor replied with a half-smile. 'If he did take . . . a touch too much, the post-mortem would show it.'

'Oh, Father wouldn't have risked a serious overdose. Much too fond of life for that. And fit for his age.' The man who so resembled the old man in the picture with Kate, and who had so clearly identified himself as that man's son, as well as Kate's husband, now shook his head. 'Funny, Kate's been complaining for years because he wouldn't hand over the business to me. Now it'll all be mine, and we can sell it, and live abroad as Kate wants, but I'm going to miss him like anything. I loved my father very much.'

This patently genuine statement impressed Dr Chalcott, but not nearly so much as it did Mr Guttins.

'The business was run as a partnership between you and your father, Mr Hallier?' the doctor asked, conversationally.

'No. I've just been a salaried dogsbody, secretary, chauffeur, you name it. Should have made me resentful, I suppose, but it didn't. Kate found it harder to take. Especially as it seemed Father intended living for ever. And now this has happened, I can't help feeling guilty, as if—'

'He was so lively yesterday,' Kate interrupted loudly. She had moved one hand up to her shoulder to squeeze her husband's fingers, 'we wondered if the Digoxin could have been stronger than usual, didn't we Jack?'

Dr Chalcott looked across at Mr Guttins who still hadn't uttered. 'Mr Guttins here is much too careful a pharmacist to make a mistake with a prescription,' said the doctor.

'Oh, I didn't mean to suggest that,' said Kate carefully, her eyes quite dry now. 'Not precisely. But, as you said, from what's left in the bottle, my father-in-law couldn't have taken too much. All I meant was, pharmacists are such busy, over-worked people. They must make occasional mistakes, like everybody else.'

'We're all human, of course,' the doctor agreed blandly, sipping his coffee.

Kate smiled. 'And if anything goes wrong,' she went on, 'I suppose a pharmacist just gets a ticking off, doesn't he? That's only fair because of the enormous responsibility he carries every day. I mean there wouldn't be a criminal charge? Not over one professional error?'

'What are you getting at, Kate?' her husband asked, frowning.

'Nothing. Really, I just got carried away. Sorry.' She had been looking at Mr Guttins' trembling hands as he held the bottle. 'I'm sure Mr Guttins doesn't make mistakes, it was just that . . . Are you all right, Mr Guttins?' she added next, in a concerned voice, and getting up. 'You look terribly hot. Why don't you sit down? Here, let me help you off with your jacket.'